Anatomy of Thought-Fiction

CHS Report, April 2214

Anatomy of Thought-Fiction

CHS Report, April 2214

Joanna Demers

Winchester, UK
Washington, USA

First published by Zero Books, 2017
Zero Books is an imprint of John Hunt Publishing Ltd., Laurel House, Station Approach,
Alresford, Hants, SO24 9JH, UK
office1@jhpbooks.net
www.johnhuntpublishing.com
www.zero-books.net

For distributor details and how to order please visit the 'Ordering' section on our website.

Text copyright: Joanna Demers 2016

ISBN: 978 1 78535 381 9
978 1 78535 553 0 (ebook)
Library of Congress Control Number: 2016949326

A CIP catalogue record for this book is available from the British Library.

Design: Stuart Davies

Printed and bound by CPI Group (UK) Ltd, Croydon, CR0 4YY, UK

We operate a distinctive and ethical publishing philosophy in all
areas of our business, from our global network of authors to
production and worldwide distribution.

CONTENTS

Also by Joanna Demers

Steal This Music: How Intellectual Property Law Affects Musical Creativity. Athens, GA: University of Georgia Press, 2007.

Listening Through the Noise: The Aesthetics of Experimental Electronic Music. New York: Oxford University Press, 2010.

Drone and Apocalypse: An Exhibit Catalog for the End of the World. Winchester, UK: Zero Books, 2015.

www.joannademers.com

To I and N

The publication of this book was made possible thanks to support from the Office of the Provost and Advancing Scholarship in the Humanities and Social Sciences grant program at the University of Southern California.

The Center for Humanistic Study presents its
latest report:
"Anatomy of Thought-Fiction"
A musicologist from the early twenty-first century asks
why people believe things they know are untrue.

Published by the CHS
Los Angeles, California
Copyright, 2214

Editors' Introduction

The Center for Humanistic Study was formed in 2210 with the generous support of anonymous donors. Among the CHS's previous projects were the exhibit and accompanying catalog for *Drone and Apocalypse*, which showcased apocalyptically-themed art and drone music of the early 2000s.

The mandate of the CHS is to study the discourse of the "humanities", a collection of non-scientific disciplines such as literature, history, and philosophy that were mainstays of universities during the twentieth and the beginning of the twenty-first centuries. Until around 2040, undergraduate students could choose to major in such topics as the Victorian novel or Ancient Greek history. Such programs could not guarantee employment for their graduates, and the market demand for such degrees was generally low. The rationale for such education was that it supposedly prepared students for jobs later in life requiring historical or cultural awareness, or writing skills, or in the rarest of cases, general cultural literacy. Graduate students who chose to pursue humanistic study at the doctoral level were expected to write in an even more highly specialized form of academic prose about literature, history, art, or philosophy, and such writing was disseminated in small circles of similarly qualified scholars in the format of dissertations, articles, essays, and monographs. The general public rarely read academic publications. Most doctoral candidates in the humanities aspired to jobs as university professors, but very few succeeded in landing such positions.

The instigation for this publication was the chance discovery of a postcard sent in October 2013 to Joanna Demers, a professor of musicology at the University of Southern California. Demers was sufficiently intrigued by the postcard to refer to it in the introduction of her critique of popular music that considers the role of thought-fictions, concepts that serve a purpose even though they are known to be untrue.[1] Demers intended the book as a modern counterpart to Robert Burton's seventeenth-century compendium on depression, *The Anatomy of Melancholy*. She completed a draft of the manuscript, but the book was never published. In its conclusion, Demers expressed concerns that its emphasis on thought-fictions would place it beyond the confines of her academic discipline. Yet for Demers, thought-fictions were central not only to her immediate musicological inquiry, but to the flagging state of the humanities, which even by the early 2010s were already under fire from university administrators and boards of trustees across North America. Many called for the elimination of humanities programs, citing the teetering global economy and the need for young adults to choose stable employments. Demers argued that humanists made themselves easy targets for criticism. A glutted job market forced aspiring professors, particularly those at the early stages of their careers, to publish fanciful speculations on the most arcane aspects of their fields. Academic writing had so detached itself from the lived experience of scholars and the public alike that, Demers feared, it would be regarded in subsequent eras as a particularly effete form of thought-fiction. And scholarship had deteriorated to the point where authors were judged on their ability to make false premises sound true.

This sounds like the type of jeremiad that any middle-aged professor might have launched, once a more or less stable career and income had been established. The redeeming feature of Demers' manuscript is that it goes beyond merely complaining about thought-fictions. Demers situates thought-fictions in relation to a philosophical lineage she terms the "Hegelian tradition". The writers GWF Hegel, Karl Marx, and Jacques Lacan had all recognized the role of thought-fictions in philosophy, economics, and psychoanalysis, decades before Demers wrote her book. The difference between the philosophers Demers so esteemed and the academic-writing industry was not that the former abstained from thought-fictions, but rather that it fully explored the ramifications of belief in that which we know to be untrue. Academic writing, on the other hand, was quick to identify the fallacies in the thoughts of others, but operated under the tacit assumption that the beliefs of the researcher were well-founded, and never ambivalent. Demers proposed a modest first corrective by calling attention to several thought-fictions that contemporary popular musicians and listeners promulgated. She organized these thought-fictions into two contradictory positions: that music was alive, and that music was dying out.

There is no doubt that this is an odd book. Demers slides between personal and scholarly writing seemingly without transition, and at times seems guilty of the overspecialization and quibbling she faults in academics. But these quirks are intelligible if one considers the larger cultural context. Social media and the over-democratization of the political process had, by the early twenty-first century, eroded the already thinning distinctions between the private and public. And among Demers' peer group, which prided itself on its level of education and its progressive social values, belief of any sort, whether religious or otherwise, was suspect. The act of admitting belief was already risky, but to admit an imperfect, ambivalent belief was downright dangerous. For behold what belief reaped: intolerance, persecution, prejudice – all these were standard fare for Demers' day. The humanistic disciplines claimed to fight these ills by seeking reality amid belief – in short, to do the work of the sciences by seeking the objective truth. By comparison, Demers suggests a dark path to knowledge, one that saw belief for the messy bundle of emotions it is.

We have published Demers' manuscript in its original version, adding our own footnotes (marked "Editors' Note") only as appropriate, and a Postscript.

Abstract

Style has traditionally been regarded as a mechanism for conveying knowledge and guiding expectations. Style can be said to be the defining attributes of a specific work, artist, or genre. It is what a musical work or artist sounds like. The status of style in popular music currently resides in a state of great flux, even volatility. Spotify, for instance, claims as one of its goals the obsolescence of genre, and encourages subscribers to broaden their listening choices beyond the confines of genre through curating track-lists for particular activities and times of day.[2] We are now several decades into the era of artistic chameleons ranging from David Bowie and Scott Walker to Kanye West and Taylor Swift, for whom a stylistic or genre shift is as easy as a wardrobe change. And thanks in part to the retromania[3] that makes supposedly old musical styles fashionable once again, style has become the latest battleground for litigation, as stylistic markers that never before qualified for copyright protection now count as intellectual property. Style has become a quantifiable phenomenon; experts in music informational retrieval (MIR) now map changes in style and genre on the basis of harmonic and timbral characteristics. Researchers are even framing style in terms of Darwinian evolution. These divergent and, at times, fanciful ways of thinking underscore the centrality of style in pop-music discourse. They also suggest that we are no longer entirely sure what style in popular music means. Through thinking in terms of such "musical fictions" – and through inter-mittently believing them – we evade the existential reality of style, the fact that it no longer means very much.

Anatomy of Thought-Fiction proposes a method for unraveling the knots that complicate our understanding of pop-music style. Part I introduces the category of the thought-fiction: a concept that serves some purpose even though it is known to be untrue.

A defining characteristic of today's popular music is its promulgation of beliefs that, although recognizably fallacious, are received as truth by artists, listeners, and entrepreneurs. Drawing from the philosophy of Hegel and Marx as well as Lacan's psychoanalytic theory, this section distinguishes thought-fictions from metaphors, which are useful, false concepts that are always acknowledged as false. Unlike metaphors, the thought-fictions surrounding pop style are subtle because they can be identified as false or believed as truth; they can even be believed and discounted simultaneously. I present a preliminary example of a thought-fiction taken from Greil Marcus' *Lipstick Traces* (on the heroism of punk performance) before introducing the two thought-fictions that guide the subsequent essays: "Music is alive", and "Music can die out". Both fictions have developed as a result of the confusion over style. I conclude by reflecting on how we can discern fictions, even while keeping in mind that we can never exorcise them from our thinking about music.

Part II explores the ways in which stylistic proliferation causes us to conceive of pop music as alive. Musicians and philosophers treat sounds in genres like electronica as if they possessed the capacity to suffer. Researchers are applying theories of biological evolution to explain changes in pop style. And recent developments in technology and intellectual-property law beg the same sorts of metaphysical questions that dog discussions of species classification. These various fictions underscore the fact that, for many within and outside of academia, music itself is increasingly an object of biological discourse.

Part III interrogates how discourses of stylistic scarcity and regression cause us to perceive pop music as undergoing extinction. David Bowie's recent passing has highlighted how his approach toward stylistic change is no longer possible today. While the present or the future used to be preferred topics for pop songs, many artists today prefer to retreat to the past – not some supposedly authentic past, but an explicitly fantastical, made-up past – with apparently no sense of irony. And because of drastic changes in how music is produced, distributed, consumed, and sold, we have embraced a view that pop is an endangered species.

The Conclusion considers the consequences, both desirable and otherwise, of thought-fictions, and suggests a way to live with them, but not under them.

Robert Burton wrote his *Anatomy of Melancholy* as a scholarly work that defined the illness and explored its treatments. But Burton also admitted that he wrote about melancholy because he himself suffered from it. *Anatomy of Thought-Fiction* is meant in kind, as a scholarly dissection of a phantasm, even a mental illness, from which I suffer. For I too believe in ideas that I know are false.

Part I

Thought-Fictions and Musical Style

Postcards and Thought-Fictions

In October 2013 I received a postcard sent from Bangalore, India. To this day, it remains a mystery to me. The sender's cursive is expansive and lovely, and seems familiar. But try as I might, I cannot make out the signature underneath the salutation ("With best wishes") that would identify the sender. Three five-rupee stamps depict scenes from Jayadeva's epic poem, the *Geetagovinda*. The stamps form an upper border over the handwriting that, curiously, appears in three colors of ink: pink (for "AIR mail"); light blue (for "With best wishes – [and the sender's name, presumably] – 21/10 [something illegible] Rd – B'lore"); and dark blue for my name and address. This side of the postcard is, for me, a delightful little enigma. The provenance of the card seems just beyond my reach, as if merely one more autographical clue would reveal the sender to be an old friend or teacher, someone whom I know.

The mystery only increases when I consider what is printed on the other side of the postcard. It is a flow chart with text in seven colors. The heading states, "M = ER^2". This equation is written out in the following line as "Memory = Emotion x Rhyme x Rhythm". Surrounding these four words are terms and phrases such as "Cerebellum Basal Ganglia", "Sub-conscious or implicit memory", and "Five senses". These various pronouncements are entangled in a web of arrows and text boxes that refer to chemicals ("Dopamine", "Oxytocin", "Serotonin", and "Endorphins") and areas of the brain. Elsewhere on the card appear statements like "Music is in the genes", "Amygdala & Accumbens (ventral striatum) (Musical emotion)", and "Lights upto [sic] Fear & Music on scans". Near the bottom, the postcard declares that "Reticular formation may be the prime mover of 'Consciousness' 'Arousal' and 'Emotion' because of its many connections especially to the Automatic & Endocrine systems. It is the great 'Unifier' as is 'Music'."

This thicket of interlocking branches and arrows makes any of my interpretations provisional at best. The postcard would seem to claim that music stimulates the areas of the brain that regulate memory and affective response. The visual surfeit is pleasantly esoteric for my taste, but its quirks notwithstanding, the postcard contends that music is a measurable stimulus, a phenomenon that exerts quantifiable effects on the human brain. A brief internet search indicates that the text draws from the writings of an M.R. Shetty, who published a few books of poetry and rhyming couplets.[4] It may be that the sender is himself M.R. Shetty, but I will probably never know for certain. I also do not know why I was sent this postcard. So most of what could be known about this communication will remain unknowable to me. What I do know is that I find myself disagreeing with the postcard's message. Music is more complicated than the flow chart lets on, because so much of music's affect depends on acculturation, education, and environment, variables that are challenging enough to describe on their own, let alone as they interact with cognitive phenomena. Still, the message of the postcard is hard for me to discount entirely. If its purpose is to convince readers that music affects our emotions, that music can trigger and aid memory, then despite knowing otherwise, I believe what this postcard says. We can all think of examples in our personal lives that would support such a claim. And if the postcard's pseudo-scientific rhetoric strikes me as tenuous, it doesn't matter, for I have accepted this message as a beautiful fiction, an untruth I believe in order to approach the considerably more difficult questions of *how* music affects our emotions and cognition, and *why* it does so in a manner that is distinct for each listener.

Other disciplines are marked by these same fault-lines separating science from the arts and humanities. Aesthetics acknowledges that music can trigger memory and induce affective response, but its claims are often transcendental (meaning applicable to all listeners, or all listeners of a particular type) and bypass issues of physiology, cognition, or culture. At its weakest, aesthetics behaves like the stereotype some non-philosophers have conceived of it: elitist and effete, based on armchair speculation. Neuroscience, on the other hand, sets out to explain empirically how music affects cognition, but its focus on cerebral function runs the risk of overlooking the effects of culture, history, economics, politics, and (especially!) aesthetics. At its least convincing, neuroscience reduces listening to input and output streams connected to the black box that is the mind, which itself is reduced to a particularly complex computer. My mysterious postcard deploys a peculiar assemblage of esoteric aesthetics and neuroscience. Although I know that '$M=ER^{2'}$' is mathematically incoherent since the postcard defines 'R' as two distinct variables, I can nonetheless momentarily indulge in this thought-fiction to go where the rival disciplines of aesthetics and neuroscience are unable to follow.

I use the term "thought-fiction" purposefully to refer to a concept that serves a purpose even though it is known to be untrue. When we are enthralled by a beautiful sky at dusk, for instance, we tend to think of sunsets as the moment when the sun slowly descends behind the western horizon. No matter our level of education or age, it is easy to conceive of a sunset as the product of the sun's, rather than Earth's, movement because we cannot feel Earth's rotation. Sunsets stand at the junction of what we know to be true and that which we believe out of habit or convenience. Our ordinary, unreflected experience of sunsets amounts to a convention we know to be contrary to fact, yet that concurs with the way we perceive our planet. In jurisprudence, there is a term to describe such situations. "Legal fictions" are statements made in legal proceedings that are acknowledged as false, but are not intended to deceive.[5] Legal fictions can be as non-descript as a "metaphorical way of expressing the truth"[6], or more purposively, can be "false statements recognized as having utility".[7] Among the most infamous of recent legal fictions is the 2010 Supreme Court decision *Citizens United v. Federal Election Commission*, which found that the First Amendment prohibits restrictions on the money that nonprofit corporations spend on election advertising.[8] Implicit (though never stated) in this ruling is the concept of corporate personhood, a legal fiction dating back to the nineteenth century that permits courts to treat corporations as persons.[9] The *Citizens United* ruling found that personhood entails protection under the First Amendment, and that limiting the amount a corporation can spend on election publicity amounts to limiting a (corporate) person's right to free expression.

The legal fiction of corporate personhood is certainly controversial, but should not give the impression that all legal fictions are cynical means to ends. A more loving legal fiction is that of adoption, since the adopted child is issued a new birth certificate that indicates only the adoptive parents. This fiction, of erasing any record of biological parents, places all rights and responsibilities with the adoptive parents. Legal fictions undergird much of modern life, amounting to crutches with which courts can approach complex issues.[10] We sometimes acknowledge these fictions as metaphors, and at other times, we simply accept them as truth. At such moments, the fiction resembles philosophy, a way of making sense of a baffling world. The fictions common in courtrooms are by no means the only sort of thought-fictions. Most of us have acted at one time or another as if we were the center of the universe, or would live forever, or enjoyed complete control over our lives. Most of us entertain these and other innumerable fictions. We may even momentarily forget what we know, at which point the thought-fiction becomes myth or ideology or delusion. As David Foster Wallace put it, "a huge percentage of the stuff that I tend to be automatically certain of is, it turns out, totally wrong and deluded".[11] But as much as fictions may permeate human cognition in general, they are especially prevalent, indeed unavoidable and indispensable, in our ways of thinking about music. They are the conditions for the possibility of musical thought, which is an obvious nod to Kant's conditions for the possibility of experience. Kant explained that anything that appears to consciousness does so through the conditions of space and time. I argue here that anything that we presume to know about pop music presents itself to us through thought-fictions. There is no way around them.

Musical Fictions of the Past

Let's look at some of the thought-fictions that have received sustained attention over the past two decades.

The acousmatic / reduced listening – The acousmatic is defined as a situation in which the site or provenance of sound is hidden from view.[12] The tension of acousmatic situations often results from the chasm separating the phenomenal source of a sound (say, Scarlett Johansson in the 2013 film *Her*) from the presumed source of the sound (according to the plot of *Her*, an invisible yet omnipresent operating system). However much the main character Theodore (played by Joaquin Phoenix) knows that the breathy voice can never be corporeal, he falls in love with that voice, and ascribes to it all the emotion and physical allure of a real woman. The acousmatic is a collision between the unknown and the imagined, or in the case of *Her*, the known and the desired. *Musique concrète*-originator Pierre Schaeffer was the first to theorize the acousmatic and proposed *reduced listening*, an ascetic practice of denial whereby we embrace an untruth of an acousmatic, unknown sound source, even if we really do in fact know that we are hearing a train or a bell.

The fiction in the acousmatic and reduced listening is that we can halt or momentarily suspend our biologically-determined faculty of identifying what we hear. Michel Chion, drawing on empirical knowledge of film sound, writes that it is impossible to disregard whatever we may know about a sound. But Schaeffer, electroacoustic composer Francisco López, and philosopher Roger Scruton say that we can (or, in Scruton's case, do) transcend our natural curiosity about the production of a sound to hear in it what we want to hear, and thus believe.[13]

Objecthood – The fiction of objecthood is that sound or music can be treated as a voluminous body.[14] Physics demonstrates that sound is ephemeral, composed of air vibrations that must dissipate, and although sound can be documented through notation or even inscribed onto a phonograph, the same sound can never be heard twice. Yet because phonography first enabled sound to be represented onto tangible objects like disks and tape, the twentieth century was rife with metaphors likening sounds to voluminous objects. Schaeffer focuses his discussion of sounds that can be divorced from their context and source, and christens such phenomena "sound objects" (*objets sonores*). After Schaeffer, it was taken for granted that such sound objects possessed attributes normally associated with three-dimensional objects: presence, plasticity, even tangibility.

Architecture – Closely related to the fiction of music's objecthood, the fiction of music as architecture imbues music with structural characteristics. Students of medieval music are familiar with Edgar Sparks' metaphor likening the tenor cantus firmus in a three- or four-voice composition to a scaffold upon which ornate melodies in the upper voices hang like garlands.[15] The "scaffolding" in Sparks' fiction is the relationship between the tenor and the other voices, an incipiently harmonic process in which the pitches of a plainchant determine vertical sonorities for the whole composition. Perhaps because musicologists have historically tended to admire architecture, Sparks and others have relied on the scaffolding metaphor to argue that Renaissance polyphony was a quasi-architectural practice. Christopher Page interrogates this passion on the part of twentieth-century musicologists for "architectonic" metaphors that rationalize late medieval music. Page contrasts twentieth-century fantasies about medieval esotericism with what were, in fact, no-nonsense rejections of such esotericism. As Page points out, early fourteenth-century theorist Johannes de Grocheio tartly quipped about Boethius' *musica humana*, the supposed harmony of the human body, "Who has heard a constitution sounding?"[16] For Page, discarding images of a romantic Middle Ages demands that we divest ourselves of the musical fictions that, over time, risk congealing into received fact. More recently, Alexander Rehding and Lydia Goehr have traced conceptions of German symphonic and operatic music as monumental, weighty, and dignified, all qualities also attributed to state buildings.[17]

Movement – Here, the fiction could be that music could elicit bodily movement in performers or listeners, or that something in music itself, whether rhythm, pitch, or timbre, moves.[18] Scruton, for instance, conceives of the second theme of the last movement of Brahms' Second Piano Concerto in B flat major, op. 83 as being traded back and forth between piano and orchestra: "Each note follows in sequence as though indifferent to the world of physical causes, and responding only to its predecessor and to the force that it inherits from the musical line."[19]

* *

This is by no means a complete list of musical fictions or scholarship devoted to them. But we can still cull one useful observation from these fictions: music is an *intentional object*, the term Franz Brentano employs to describe the object about which we think.[20] Without thought, any sort of music is just an assortment of sounds that may happen to be either improvised or planned, yet are nonetheless just sounds. But with thought, these sounds signify, point beyond themselves, and affect listener behavior. Scruton provides one of the most refreshingly honest acknowledgements of musical fictions. Our very definition of music is mutable and subjective, he writes. And however we choose to distinguish between music and non-musical sound, that distinction is not a disinterested accident, but rather, "a decision made with a purpose in mind."[21] Scruton's frank acceptance of the inevitability of musical fictions is one I share, and will advocate throughout this book.

Scholarly writing is by no means the only breeding ground for musical fictions. One of the most famous musical fictions is also perhaps the loveliest: "the little phrase" in Vinteuil's violin sonata, a work that plays a critical role in the first volume of Marcel Proust's *In Search of Lost Time*. This little phrase is a leitmotif that, in the mind of the main character Charles Swann, anticipates and embodies his love affair with Odette de Crécy. Proust bestows on Swann a double awareness, of both the significance of this musical passage in relation to his romance as well as the falsity of that significance:

> But ever since, more than a year, before, discovering to him many of the riches of his own soul, the love of music had, for a time at least, been born in him, Swann had regarded musical *motifs* as actual ideas, of another world, of another order, ideas veiled in shadow, unknown, impenetrable [380] to the human mind, but none the less perfectly distinct from one another, unequal among themselves in value and significance.[22]
>
> [...]
>
> So Swann was not mistaken in believing that the phrase of the

sonata really did exist. Human as it was from this point of view, it yet belonged to an order of supernatural beings whom we have never seen, but whom, in spite of that, we recognize and acclaim with rapture when some explorer of the unseen contrives to coax one forth, to bring it down, from that divine world to which he has access, to shine for a brief moment in the firmament of ours.[23]

There are few things as pleasantly melancholic as the music we associate with a failed romance. But Scruton refers to the fictions he brings up as *metaphors*, not fictions. Why then do I call Swann's little phrase a musical fiction rather than simply a metaphor? What distinguishes musical fictions from metaphors about music?

Scruton defines metaphor as "deliberate application of a term or phrase to something that is known not to exemplify it".[24] And this definition concurs with Fuller's definition of a legal fiction, an untrue concept used intentionally (and without mischief or intent to deceive) to achieve some goal. Both Scruton and Fuller base their respective definitions on a sober, measured awareness of the implications and limits of a thought-fiction. But this is not always the case, for musical fictions excel at camouflaging themselves amid musical knowledge and certainty. While it is certainly true that we may at times be aware of fictions as fictions, at other times, fictions may assume the guise of undisputed truth. We then will look not only to the prosaic nature of musical fictions, but also to the reasons why we at times *choose* to believe them, and why we may even forget their fictive nature.

Acknowledging Thought-Fictions

For after all, those who write about music often err by assuming an epistemology of conviction. Whatever we supposedly believe about music – that it represents identity, that it encodes messages, that it is the highest of arts, that it is purchasable property, that it epitomizes cultural values – we supposedly believe it in a way that is uncomplicated and certain. Listeners may be right or wrong about what they believe, but music-writing for the large part takes for granted that listeners are convinced that they believe the truth. But we all know of examples in daily life where belief is far from monochromatic. We may for the most part believe, for instance, in the stability of the banking system, yet we may be afflicted with unspoken fears when we put hard-earned money in savings. We may be nominally religious or atheist, and yet be momentarily afflicted with doubt as to the validity of our positions. I believe in the value of my work as a professor, yet I also know that what I do will change nothing in the world. Thought can certainly exist as matter-of-fact belief, but can also take the form of premises we only half-believe, or believe depending on mitigating circumstances. As the essays below will explain, we can even believe things we simultaneously acknowledge as false.

Music-writing may not attend to the possibility for ambivalence in belief, but the Hegelian tradition speaks a great deal about this issue. My methodology for this book is to take inspiration from a discourse stretching from GWF Hegel through Karl Marx to Jacques Lacan. These three writers talk at great length about the overlaps, slippages, and mutual dependence between thought and reality, categories that the Continental philosophical tradition had previously cordoned off from one another. Hegel, Marx, and Lacan will serve as mentors throughout this book, because their reflections on being and thought, on fetishism and ideology, and on disavowal furnish us with indispensable tools for fleshing out the category of the thought-fiction. It is naturally no coincidence that Marx and Lacan were both assiduous readers of Hegel. Let me thus begin with a summary of Hegel's rupture of the divisions between the subject and the object as well as between thought and being. I will then proceed to how Marx and

Lacan imported to economics and psychoanalysis, respectively, Hegel's assault on these walls separating supposed fiction from reality.

Hegel is an eminently suitable philosopher by which to orient this discussion. Coming of age at the beginning of the nineteenth century in Germany, he was ideally positioned to assess the French Revolution, the subsequent tyrant Napoleon, and the ascendance of modern European states. Hegel was also the most successful of the first generation of philosophers to respond to Immanuel Kant's system, especially as set out in his *Critique of Pure Reason* (1781), which effectively dismantled metaphysics by asserting that human reason was incapable of either proving or denying the existence of God, among other questions on the nature of the universe. Hegel's preoccupations remain eerily relevant today. He anticipated vital materialism, which we'll consider in "Suffering Music", in regarding inorganic natural material as possessing spirit. He also paved the way for postmodernist critiques of epistemology by arguing that thought is intrinsic to, rather than separate from, existence. At the risk of reducing Hegel's prolific contributions to a pithy one-liner, Hegel demonstrates that the guiding binaries in Western philosophy are not binary opposites, but rather interlinked and interdependent moments of dialectic.

Dialectic is central to a thought-fiction, after all. For in dialectic, two concepts simultaneously oppose and sustain one another. As explained by Stanley Rosen, the dialectic of being and thought entails that "everything is thinkable or intelligible because there is an identity within difference of being and thinking".[25] The dialectic in a thought-fiction is between belief and reality, which are simultaneously identical and distinct. Admittedly, Hegel is famous, even notorious, for spinning out his theory of dialectic into nearly all facets of experience, from human development and politics to science and religion. The dialectic most relevant to musical fictions is the central dialectic of Hegel's aesthetic theory: that art both reveals truth and is a falsehood. Prior to Hegel, Western aesthetic theory from Plato through Kant placed art beneath nature. For Plato, the best that can be expected of art is that it present an imperfect copy of an ideal.[26] Much later, Kant's anecdote of the musician and the nightingale echoes Plato; a human imitation of birdsong would seem tasteless to our ears, and is disappointing when compared to its source.[27] Plato and Kant both impose on art the obligation of fidelity; art is only as good as its ability to imitate reality. But Hegel counters that art's merit lies precisely in its ability to transcend nature, to create new worlds with inert material from the natural world. Art can thus "unveil truth"[28] that is latent, and yet does so through being "deception".[29] This uneasy teetering between lie and truth will underpin the category of a musical fiction.

Marx describes *Capital* as a scientific study of industrial economics, specifically the phenomenon whereby the sale of commodities generates surplus-value, or value above the original exchange value. This transformation can be summed up with Marx's equation, $M = C = M'$, whereby the capitalist pays money to acquire a commodity, and then sells it for a higher price. The difference between M' and M is surplus-value or capital, and results from labor-power, not from inflation or appreciation. Marx demonstrates that workers generate surplus-value after they have worked enough hours in a given day to pay for their subsistence, calculated as wages. Thus, in a work-day of, say, twelve hours, the worker generates enough labor by the end of, say, ten hours to pay his day's wages. The remaining two hours of the shift generate revenue that goes exclusively to the capitalist, who creates wealth from the unpaid two hours of this and many other workers.

Marx leaves no doubt as to his opinion of this exploitation of unpaid labor. It is unjust, and gives rise to poverty, squalid and overcrowded housing, illness and workplace accidents, sexual exploitation of women and children, intellectual and moral deprivation, and the dissolution of familial and communal bonds. Thus, one of the goals of *Capital* is to dissect the thought-fictions that make such exploitation possible. For, Marx contends, neither workers nor capitalists would accept this system if they were brought to see its true nature. The commodity is anointed with "metaphysical subtleties and theological niceties"[30] that would claim to explain why, for instance, a pair of ripped jeans could be sold new for $100. The magic or fetishism, as Marx terms it, of commodities is that they render natural, and thus invisible and immune to questioning, the social relations that make production of those jeans possible.[31] Exchange-value represents the transformation of the commodity, a product of labor, into a "hieroglyphic"[32] price, an arbitrary and "purely ideal or notation form".[33] But here, Marx pointedly calls out the thought-fiction as an open secret: "Every owner of commodities knows that he is nowhere near turning them into gold when he has given their value the form of a price or of imaginary gold, and that it does not require the tiniest particle of real gold to give a valuation in gold of millions of pounds' worth of commodities."[34] Awareness of the fiction is a luxury reserved for capitalists, since workers are too alienated from the labor process to realize how little control they exert over their work. They are struggling merely to survive.

Capital begins with the exchange of a nameless commodity. But after this nondescript beginning, Marx fairly peppers biological metaphors throughout *Capital*'s first volume: the exchange process that transforms commodities from having no use-value to positive use-value is "metabolism"[35]; value acquires the ability to add value to itself, bringing "forth living offspring, or at least [laying] golden eggs".[36] There are also supernatural metaphors: labor "raises the means of production from the dead"[37], creating new products out of old techniques, materials, and equipment. These resurrected products receive new value through "metempsychosis", or reincarnation that "takes place, as it were, behind the back of the actual labor in progress".[38] And capital itself is a vampire that "lives only by sucking living labor, and lives the more, the more labor it sucks".[39] Crucially, Marx maintains that capitalists *choose* to believe in the alchemical and occult qualities of commodity exchange: "the love of profit induces an easy belief in such miracles [...] there is no lack of sycophantic doctrinaires to prove their existence..."[40] Like an auteur director of 1970s cinema, Marx ends by giving us a far broader and bleaker perspective than the neutral formula with which he began. The political economist, a propagandist of capital, perpetuates the fiction that capitalism manifests the values of private property: that it is an inherently just system predicated on the worker's control over his labor. This is the fiction necessary to keep the machine functioning: "To this ready-made world of capital, the political economist applies the notions of law and of property inherited from a pre-capitalist world, with all the more anxious zeal and all the greater unction, the more the facts cry out in the face of his ideology."[41]

Marx will be helpful throughout this discussion for his scrupulous attestation of the true nature of thought-fictions. As the essays below will make clear, it is all too easy for us to pinpoint what initially is clearly a thought-fiction – say, that music styles evolve or that hiphop is dead – and then promptly to forget or ignore what is fictive about the concept. When this occurs, the fiction congeals into received opinion or convention. Marx, however, always spotlights the magical thinking in commodity fetishism, the uncanniness of likening labor process to the undead. Marx thus provides us with a point of orientation amid shifting sands of reality and fantasy.

Lacan's career at times paralleled Hegel's. Both succeeded in drastically redirecting their respective disciplines, Hegel through his simultaneous validation and critique of Kant, Lacan through his simultaneous validation and critique of Freud. Lacan's writings are today often encountered as free-standing philosophy or critical theory, and they can function well enough in that capacity. But it is important to appreciate the ambitus that Lacan's thought spans. On the one hand, he attended Alexandre Kojève's Hegel seminars during the 1930s, and thus benefitted from a thorough grounding in Hegelian thought. From these classes, Lacan drew his lifelong focus on the master/slave dialectic that Hegel expounds in his *Phenomenology of Spirit*[42], a relationship in which dominant and servile subjects both experience desire. Lacan abstracts from these Hegelian studies the argument that any intimate relationship is a struggle for recognition, and also, a struggle to be desired. On the other hand, Lacan was trained in the late 1920s as a psychiatrist, and practiced in that capacity for some years, treating patients who suffered from paranoid psychosis. He became a proponent of Freud's psychoanalysis in the 1930s, proclaiming that he was leading the discipline to a rediscovery of Freud's ideas. Lacan began offering seminars in 1951 in which he unpacked his particular take on psychoanalysis; by 1953, the seminars became public and were documented in various collections that literary theorists and art historians have since regarded as a singular critical apparatus.

I want to focus on one particular element in Lacan's vast corpus because of its direct relevance to this book, the concept of *disavowal*. To preface, Freud in 1925 wrote a brief essay entitled *"Verneinung"* (Negation), which relates that a patient will often deny information that surfaces in the course of therapy.[43] Freud states that disavowed information is valuable because it first emerges when the patient is faced with an uncomfortable truth that he previously repressed into his subconscious. The act of negating or disavowing the truth is thus an important intermediary step in treatment, for it is the moment when repressed desire enters the conscious. The patient still denies the information, but at least the information is now accessible to therapeutic examination. Interestingly, Freud expresses this in Hegelian terms; he writes, "Negation is a way of taking cognizance of what is repressed; indeed it is already a *lifting* of the repression, though not, of course, an acceptance of what is repressed."[44] In the original German text, Freud uses the word *"Aufhebung"* (translated into English as "lifting"), the word Hegel uses to describe sublation, or the simultaneous repressing and uplifting that is inherent to the dialectic.

Lacan invited Jean Hyppolite, a fellow participant in Kojève's Hegel seminars as well as the first to translate Hegel's *Phenomenology of Spirit* into French, to write an introduction to Freud's "Negation" that he then discusses in his first Seminar.[45] Hyppolite's essay hones in on Freud's use of *"Aufhebung"*, saying that disavowal consists of negating, suppressing, and conserving all at once.[46] Lacan in turn makes central to his philosophy this contradictory relationship with the truth. To cite just one example, Lacan refers to the chorus in Sophocles' *Antigone* as the force that does the feeling for the audience: "Your emotions are taken charge of by the healthy order displayed on the stage. The Chorus takes care of them. The emotional commentary is done for you [...] Therefore, you don't have to worry; even if you don't feel anything, the Chorus will feel it in your stead."[47] So, Lacan expands Freud's understanding of disavowal, initially a concept specific to psychoanalysis, to refer to any situation in which we may actually displace emotion or belief onto another entity.

Lacan will complement Marx's sober diagnosis of the fiction in thought-fictions. For Lacan points out the central role of belief in thought-fictions, and the fact that we disavow belief by dismissing it as merely convention or custom. Lacan will thus remind us not to remain jaded about the sometimes outlandish things that we claim only to half-believe about music. As Part III will illustrate, pop music is full of implicit and explicit statements as to the impending extinction of rock or hiphop, or even the pop recording industry altogether. Seasoned observers of the industry would be right to point out that such statements are not new, and indeed are part of the myth-making machine that drives pop, belying its reliance on the past. That said, Lacan cautions against shrugging off the ramifications of fictions we only half-believe, or only believe out of custom. The belief in the imminent death of hiphop or commercial recordings is exerting a real effect on the decisions of artists and listeners. We need to reclaim our disavowed beliefs about pop if we are to understand its perennial changes as something more than arbitrary change of taste.

Fictions about Pop Style

Style in pop music used to be considered more or less stable, cemented to an artist or album or song. But today, style has become something of a variable, even a "manipulable". This possibility was first broached when sampling allowed instantaneous importation of one recording into another. Sampling enabled collisions of styles that had never before commingled: rock with rap in Run DMC's version of "Walk This Way" (1986); metal with rap in Public Enemy's "Bring The Noise" (1987); Bollywood with rap in Truth Hurts' "Addictive" (2002). Now, the affordances of technology, sampling and otherwise, have made possible rapid stylistic changes within tracks of any genre. Just think of Beyoncé's 2016 surprise album *Lemonade*, which NPR praised for demonstrating the artist's control over genre transformations within the album, and even within a single song.[48]

This observation is just the beginning. Because style is so much more vigorously exploited today, what we believe about style surpasses anything that we used to believe about style. The goal of this inquiry is not to debunk thought-fictions about style. Rather, my guiding principle is adapted from Hegel's philosophy of art[49]: musical style is comprised of both sounds and what we believe about those sounds. In other words, style itself is a thought-fiction. And this is not an undesirable state of affairs.

Part II, "Music Is Alive", considers attempts to render music into an object of biological discourse. I begin with recent tracks that treat sound as alive, non-human, and capable of suffering. These tracks can be profitably understood as practicing what theorists like Paul Virilio, Tim Morton, and Reza Negarestani regard as consequences of eternal warfare and environmental depravation. Human culture has sustained multiple blows to its sense of preeminence since the eighteenth century. And whereas traditional musicology frequently conceives of musical works as props for human subjectivity, pop styles that rely on sampling and audio treatment (particularly hiphop, electronic dance music [EDM], and electronica) propose an alternative biological presence that is not a mouthpiece for humanity. I then turn toward attempts to explain musical history and development in terms of Darwin's theory of evolution. Tomlinson[50], for instance, characterizes the rise of musicality as intrinsic to *homo sapiens'* development, and Mauch et al.[51] invoke evolution to assert that American pop has undergone three revolutions. This fiction is premised on analogies linking stylistic change to variables determining the diversity of a species' characteristics. Thus, a prehistoric primate's mimicking of the sound of a bird is explained as an example of a species adapting itself to its environment; variations within a musical style are rationalized as "mutations" that, if successful, eventually become intrinsic to that style. I conclude Part II with a discussion of musical phylogeny in the aftermath of the 2015 judgment against Robin Thicke and Pharrell Williams for their hit "Blurred Lines", which was deliberately modeled on the "feel" of Marvin Gaye's "Got To Give It Up" (1977). The "Blurred Lines" verdict proclaims that the essence of a musical work can now be anything idiomatic: a timbre, a percussion pattern, even a style. This fiction disrupts a century-old understanding of musical works as being defined primarily by melody and lyrics rather than style, and threatens to stifle the one remaining legal and free avenue for creative reference open to musicians. The verdict also sets into motion a fiction that ratio-nalizes pop-music styles in terms of phylogeny, or the evolu-tionary history of a species of organism. The seemingly unrelated movement toward copyrighting stylistic elements and *even style itself* forces pop musicians and listeners to confront questions that also emerge in evolutionary biology: what is it that defines an individual, whether that individual is an organism or a musical work? What defines a species, and what defines a musical style? And what about an individual's genetic makeup should be patentable, just as what about a musical work should be copyrightable?

Part III, "Music Can Die Out", investigates the fiction that various aspects of the pop-music industry are becoming extinct. I begin with "What We Lost in Losing Bowie", which argues that the defining trait of his career was less his rapid and frequent stylistic metamorphoses than the consistency of his underlying persona. Bowie's oeuvre upheld the old definition of style, that it was comprised of secondary qualities surrounding the essence or substance of a work or artist. What we lost in losing Bowie is not, as the thought-fiction suggests, a master of stylistic reinvention, for many artists today engage in the same sort of stylistic change. Rather, we lost a clear distinction between style and substance, because style today has in effect become substance. I conclude this essay with the complementary example of Scott Walker, who, like Bowie, made stylistic reinvention central to his artistic persona. In "A Society for Creative Anachronism", I turn to artists who create fantasy worlds premised on the interchangeability and immediate availability of styles. We listen here to Actually Huizenga and The KLF, and also consider the nostalgia for a fictional history of cassette tape. In "Post-Genres", I ruminate on the types of music supposedly generated by a genre's demise; we'll listen here to post-rock and post-hiphop. Post-genres "work" by positing the extinction of their parent genre. Finally, "Acquisitive Philanthropy" questions the fiction that purchasing music is an act of charity. This fiction has its roots in the crisis of the early 2000s, when online piracy threatened the collapse of the record industry. While total recording sales today are less than half of what they were a decade ago, the industry continues to function. There are still major and independent record labels, iTunes continues to turn a profit, Spotify's revenue is rising, and most surprisingly, many listeners purchase music knowing that they could easily and legally listen to it for free. The industry's resilience is due to savvy adjustments to its business and marketing models. Chief among these adjustments is the cultivation of what I dub "acquisitive philanthropy", the belief that listeners who choose to pay for music become patrons of the arts. The financial transaction, which used to be a more or less mandatory condition for acquiring music, has been transformed into a voluntary and ennobling act that benefits artists, purchasers, and society at large.

Rock and Performing Belief

I want now to present a first example of a thought-fiction in pop music. This fiction broadcasts its ambiguity, the slippage between musicians' awareness of the falsity of, and sincere investment in, the fiction. It comes to us from an essay published in 1982 in *Artforum* by Kim Gordon, guitarist and bassist of Sonic Youth. In the course of her observations about club venues in New York, Gordon writes:

> People pay to see others believe in themselves. Maybe people don't know whether they can experience the erotic or whether it exists only in commercials; but on stage, in the midst of rock 'n' roll, many things happen and anything can happen, whether people come as voyeurs or come to submit to the moment. As a performer you sacrifice yourself, you go through the motions and emotions of sexuality for all the

people who pay to see it, to believe that it exists. The better and more convincing the performance, the more an audience can identify with the exterior involved in such an expenditure of energy. Performers appear to be submitting to the audience, but in the process they gain control of the audience's emotions. They begin to dominate the situation through the awe inspired by their total submission to it. Someone who works hard at his or her job is not going to become a "hero", but may make just enough money to be able to afford to be liberated temporarily through entertainment. A performer, however, as the hero, will be paid for being sexually uncontrolled, but will still be at the mercy of the clubs and the way the media shapes identity. How long can someone continue to exert intensity before it becomes mannered and dishonest?[52]

Gordon is able to infuse the passage with the melancholy ambivalence that is shared by the rock musicians and audiences she describes. The audience may admit what it already knows, that the spectacle is a performance and, therefore, contrived, even artificial. Or, the audience may believe that the "erotic" (here, an unfettered expression of belief and pleasure) is real but forever off-limits to the likes of them, the worker bees who will never be "heroes". Both beliefs can exist, for the rock concert is a place where prurient voyeurism and sincere belief-as-submission can occur simultaneously. Likewise, musicians are aware that they are putting on a show for the audience, they "go through the motions and emotions of sexuality", but somewhere in the course of doing so, they come to dominate those spectators to whom they submit.

Gordon's essay is full of Hegelian master/slave dialectic that would seem familiar to any participant in Kojève's seminar. This passage ends forlornly with the premise that musicians risk losing the plot of the fiction, forgetting that they once believed in it. The chronology of events is important here: in Gordon's account, the fantasy exists at the beginning, when the prospect of performed sexual license is exciting. The fantasy arises from the condition of uncertainty and instability that is the club, and from a certain naïve idealism about what rock performers do. Repetition and exhibitionism transform the fantasy into fiction. Note, though, that this anticlimax is absent from the most well-known citation of Gordon's essay, found in Greil Marcus' *Lipstick Traces*.[53] There, Marcus quotes only two sentences from Gordon in a passage that states that punk musicians dare to do what the rest of us, with our petty attachments, are too craven to do. This is not a surprising interpretation within the context of Marcus' beautiful elegy to the Sex Pistols and to the genre of punk. But in Marcus' paraphrase, there is no let-down, no moment of clarity when the fantasy cedes to fiction. For this reason, Marcus' invocation of Gordon is less pertinent to my investigation than Gordon's original text, which captured the epistemological doubt that is at the root of a musical fiction. By Marcus' interpretation, Sonic Youth was safely, unremarkably heroic. But Gordon lets us in on a secret: the musicians know that they are performing belief in themselves, that they in fact are pretending to believe in themselves for the purpose of entertainment. They know that what they are doing is a sort of theater, and yet they act AS IF it is true. Likewise, the audience members know that they are watching a performance, not only of punk music but of punk as a vehicle for personal conviction. And yet they act AS IF the performance is sincere, and what is more, they act AS IF they believe in the performed sincerity because it contains something they feel they lack, something they can experience voyeuristically by means of the concert. The disillusionment that Gordon describes is integral, in fact, to a musical fiction in which participants pretend to believe something they know is not true. Without saying so, Gordon's passage also reveals that the fiction in question has everything to do with style and genre. Gordon refers to the style at hand as "rock 'n' roll", but we could be forgiven for eliding, as Marcus does, Gordon's "rock 'n' roll" with punk or postpunk, which in 1982 were the analogs of 1950s rock 'n' roll: loud, rebellious, sexy, and nihilistic. The tragedy that Gordon describes is something that Marcus' gloss ignores: the premise of punk rock as a style is rebellion and sincerity, but even that premise is, after all, a performance.

Sands have shifted in the thirty-some years since Gordon published her essay. Punk has been coopted to the point of being an expedient marker of rebellion, whether in advertising, film or television, or retromaniacal music. That punk is artifice is widely known; this fiction has been tamed to the point of becoming common knowledge. But there are other, new fictions of the mind that inflect what we think about style in pop today. Subtle and easy to overlook, they can tell us as much about current anxieties over humanity's identity and future as they can about prosaic questions of music classification. But only if we choose to confront them.

Part II

Music Is Alive

Music has become an object of scientific discourse. This is not to suggest that scientists prior to the contemporary era did not research music. They did, of course, from Aristotle to Mersenne to Darwin. The shift I am describing resides in the urgency with which music is now being conceptualized as a phenomenon best studied with scientific and technical methods. There is an unspoken desire here to justify music by incorporating it with subjects traditionally interrogated through the sciences, fields like cognition, medicine, and as we'll see below, biology. Consider that one of the bestselling publications about music of the past ten years is Daniel J. Levitin's *This Is Your Brain On Music: The Science of a Human Obsession*, which profiles neuroscientific curiosities and mysteries such as how we remember music, why we tap our feet to a beat, and why we prefer some types of music to others.[54] Levitin's book belongs to a whole body of literature that explains the science of music.[55] And although Levitin's book is preeminent in this vein, there abound other scholarly works that demonstrate links between music and the sciences. Humanists are likewise embracing science as an object of historical and musicological inquiry. Georgina Born's *Rationalizing Culture* is a history and critical examination of IRCAM and postwar contemporary music, and documents composition's direct links with science and the defense industry.[56] Electronic music benefitted directly from acoustics and electronics research, and its aesthetics arguably spring from the then-novel view that music has as much in common with engineering and physics as it does with poetry or philosophy. Douglas Kahn's recent work on music and sound art inspired by natural and specifically geological forces, underscores the view that music should work alongside science to access concealed information about nature.[57]

Not everyone in academia is sanguine about the coupling of science with music. John Croft, a lecturer in composition at Brunel University in London, indicts the trend in higher education to hold the liberal and fine arts to the standards of STEM, that unsettling acronym for science, technology, engineering, and mathematics.[58] Recessions and the contracting global job market have made the choice to major in music or literature, always a dicey one, especially foolhardy. But now, even established faculty who teach the arts are expected to explain their activities as, or in terms of, scientific research. For some artists, this poses no significant burden, because their practice can be described in grant proposals and summaries of activities as exploration of unknown territory. But for composers like Croft, the pressure to make new music intelligible to administrators trained in the hard, biological, or social sciences leads to concessions of true aesthetic import. No longer is the goal to write good music, but rather to write music that makes a good grant narrative for a review panel of scientists.

Levitin's and others' research, and the realities of academia, have thus accustomed us to thinking about music in terms of science. Granted, the texts above originate in academic or research centers, and for the most part, they treat Western experimental, avant-garde, or classical music. My charge in this section is to demonstrate that pop music is also conceptualized scientifically, possessing some of the qualities that distinguish living organisms from inert matter as well as human cultural artifacts. Thinking of music as alive occurs within and outside of the academy, among musicians, listeners, and industry heads. This does not mean that we will analyze pop songs that are "about" life in any thematic sense, though there are copious examples of pop that is about nature or life, death or evolution. Instead, I argue that thinking about pop music entails a series of fictions that, when taken in sum, indicate that we consciously or otherwise conceive of music as *alive*. I do not mean this in any esoteric or hallucinogenic sense. In "Suffering Music", I uncover how electronica now deploys melody not as a mouthpiece for the artist's subjectivity, but rather as a non-human subjectivity that suffers at the hands of humans. "Change and Evolution" considers how the emerging field of music informatics retrieval applies evolutionary theory to explain stylistic change. And in "Musical Phylogeny", the same arguments against encroachments on music copyright law are used to defend against turning genetic material into intellectual property. Although no one profiled in this section might say that music is alive in so many words, and although the topic of music as a living force does not come up in discussions or song lyrics, this is not really the point. The thought-fiction that music is evolving has already passed into our cognitive background to become a not-particularly remarkable given.

It's one thing to bring up the slew of books about music as science, but quite another to claim that we believe that music is alive. How did we get here? We can begin with one of the creation myths for Western art: the Greek myth of Pygmalion and Galatea. The story is simple: Pygmalion, a brilliant, lonely sculptor, undertakes his masterpiece, a statue of a breathtakingly beautiful woman. He soon falls in love with the statue. The gods pity the artist and bestow life upon his creation, whom they name Galatea. Pygmalion kisses the statue, and its stony lips soften and warm to become the lips of a living woman. In the Greek version of this tale, Galatea is perfect because of her physical allure, but also because she is exactly the lover Pygmalion wants. Yet the myth has had enough sway to inspire G.B. Shaw's play *Pygmalion* (1913) and its subsequent adaptation as a musical, *My Fair Lady* (1956), as well as an episode of the original *Star Trek* series, "Requiem for Methuselah"(1969). In these later versions, the Galatea-figure does not acquiesce to her creator's whims quite so eagerly; she becomes an independent entity. The discipline of musicology, insofar as it subscribes to the premise that a musical work communicates, shows that it too has assimilated the fiction of the artwork as a living being. The scholarship embodying this premise is considerable and embraces diverse strategies, from those that hear in music expressions of racial, ethnic, or sexual identities, to those that hear political messages, to those that hear a self-enclosed, "purely" musical meaning, but meaning nonetheless.[59] *The axiom that music is meaningful camouflages the premise that music represents our subjectivity.* This subjectivity amounts to the thoughts and desires that we, the humans who make and listen to music, foist upon it.

In pop music, as in the arts and humanities generally, this fiction is slowly being replaced with a new one that has stemmed from shifts in philosophy, culture, and environmental conditions, and also from the growing awareness of humanity's contribution toward those conditions. These shifts read like a countdown to modern subjectivity[60]: Copernicus and Galileo demonstrate that Earth is not the center of the universe. Kant claims to bring about a "Copernican revolution" of philosophy whereby subjectivity is revealed as an obstacle for knowing things-in-themselves. Darwin shows that humans are descended from apes. Freud claims that human behavior is controlled by unconscious desires, and cites this as the third in a series of blows to humanity's sense of importance (the first two struck by Copernicus and Darwin).[61] Humanity's dawning awareness of its weakness and inconsequentiality has been accelerated by ecological crises large and small: pollution, the depletion of the ozone layer, overfishing, deforestation, genetic modification, and of course, climate change resulting from petrochemical and livestock consumption. Contemporary philosophy articulates the problems and prospects of this new landscape where humanity is only one actor among both living and non-living agents. Quentin Meillassoux and Graham Harman, for instance, write on philosophy's failure to acknowledge its own epistemological imitations.[62] And Timothy Morton argues that concepts like "nature" and "the end of the world", which relieve humanity of accountability for its actions, must be supplanted with an acknowledgment of its responsibility for global warming and environmental damage.[63] Morton has also proposed the category of the "hyperobject", an event or phenomenon of such great scale that it defies human understanding. For Morton, hyperobjects have triggered much recent art that speaks to the disruption of human dominance.

It is not enough to observe that humans have been dethroned from their illusory pride of place. The vacuum of our displacement is being filled not only by organisms (like plants or animals) easily enough described as living, but also by entities and phenomena recognized as having vital characteristics, though not alive *per se*. For the very notion of life is now highly volatile, and according to the discourse of "vital materialism", there exist valid ethical and political reasons for extending to non-living objects the label of "living".[64] The literature on this subject runs the gamut from the history of philosophy[65] to contemporary critical theory.[66] The most intriguing writings in this vein are those that use posthumanity and vital materialism as the basis for creative work. Reza Negarestani, for instance, has written a novel of sorts called *Cyclonopedia*.[67] I say "of sorts" because the novel takes the form of a notebook of cobbled scholarly essays and fragments, diary entries, and SMS conversations all centering around the Middle East. The conceit of the book is that the Middle East and oil are believed to be living, malevolent entities. The outrageousness of this claim drives various characters to madness, and Negarestani shadows this madness with his impossibly serpentine prose, full of bloated phrase constructions better suited to a doctoral dissertation. This is post-humanity in action *in an artwork*, regardless of whether the artwork succeeds in the aims the artist has set for it.

Cyclonopedia leaves no doubt that the humans who created or consume oil have also lost control of oil. The living non-living object is ungainly and unsympathetic to our desires.

Part II examines the thought-fiction that pop music is evolving in this non-human sense. Let me clarify what this fiction is not. It does not culminate in explicit statements that pop music is alive the same way that animals or plants are. Rather, like Negarestani, I rely on syllogism. We conceive of music as evolving because we believe that music has qualities normally possessed only by living matter: the capacity to feel pain ("Suffering Music"), diversity and adaptability ("Change and Evolution"), and characteristics that it passes on to its subsequent generations ("Musical Phylogeny"). Nor does Part II argue that this fiction has to do with any particular message communicated by pop music. Listeners may find references to evolution in their music, but any such meaning has no bearing on this fiction. Finally, this fiction does not argue that music is sentient, though some artists and listeners may subscribe to that view. Rather, pop is now being conceptualized as an entity with a vitality that is not human, though it originates from human actions. Pop, in other words, is a sort of nature, a nature divested of utopian fantasy.

If these are fictions, the corresponding fact at first glance would seem to be that art is not, *cannot* be alive, and thus cannot evolve in the same way as organisms. (We will discuss theories of cultural evolution in "Change and Evolution", and the differences between cultural and biological evolution.) Common sense might say that art is firmly rooted within human culture, and thus could belong neither to posthumanity nor to nature. Fact would also cordon off "nature" as a special type of life or organic entity (assuming we count stones and clouds and other non-living entities as "nature") that is nonetheless not human or artificial. But Hegel writes that art and nature are dialectically linked, for art is both distinct from, and a magical return to, nature. Hegel admits that "the work of art is certainly nothing animated, and, since there is nothing just externally alive, the living thing is higher than what is lifeless".[68] Yet art improves upon nature in that it reflects on raw materials, mediating them through Spirit. Unlike living matter, in other words, art is permanent, and enjoys a double existence as both physical and metaphysical. Art enchants not because it is natural, but because it has been made natural.[69] Artworks imbue inert, natural materials (i.e. stone, wood, canvas, even speech) with spirit; Hegel calls this "the baptism of spirit".[70] The point of this digression into Hegel is that we can choose other than to scoff at the idea that music is alive if we admit, with Hegel, Negarestani, and the other writers mentioned above, that the categories of art, life, and nature overlap when we dare to conceive of a life without humanity.

Suffering Music

Few subjects in twentieth-century music studies have received as much attention as noise. It's worth revisiting this terrain to survey what we now take for granted. At the beginning of the 1900s, there still existed the distinction between supposedly musical and non-musical sound. The barrier between these two realms came under attack when writers like Edgard Varèse, Pierre Schaeffer, John Cage, and Jacques Attali preached the intrinsic value of *all* sounds, even those maligned as noise or cacophony or detritus. This embrace of the non-musical coincided with the emergence of phonography, which permitted for the first time capture and affixing of both music and the noise previously cordoned off from music. These were heady times of ideology, and the integration of noise with musical sound was uneven in practice. Avant-gardists and experimentalists overcorrected by relying on noise to the exclusion of traditionally beautiful materials. Popular musicians tended to use noise and dissonance only coloristically to connote uprising or rebellion.

But sounds of phonographic noise appeared frequently in pop and avant-garde music, from Milan Knizak's use of damaged records and hiphop's deliberate reverse playback of records in the 1970s, to Christian Marclay's use of trampled and cracked vinyl in both recordings and installations in the 1980s. By the 1990s, noise had become a prized aesthetic object as well as a topic for critical discourse. The most influential of the interpretations of noise to emerge from this period was Kim Cascone's 2000 essay on one type of noise-filled music, "glitch".[71] Technology, Cascone's argument goes, has so permeated culture that we have nearly lost our ability to compose or even live without it. This technology is often sold to us on the basis of its unobtrusive qualities and sleek design. Noise disrupts this fantasy by reminding us of the inevitable failure that even the most advanced technologies will produce. Noise is, in other words, a means of political and artistic resistance. I added to this argument by noting several experimental electronica works that use noise to render sounds into objects, with all the associations to meaninglessness that such objecthood entails.[72] To summarize what we now commonly think about noise: the process of incorporating noise into music has been received as an expression of disillusionment with the illusory gains of technology. But artists and musicians have frequently explained the sounds of noise themselves as neutral materials, ciphers standing in for meaning rather than possessing any meaning.

This two-faceted position contains an internal contradiction ("noise is resistant, but noise means nothing") that wasn't sustainable even when it was at its most prominent in the 1990s. The latter half of this claim is specious because the very declaration of the meaninglessness of objecthood is itself a meaningful, ideologically-rooted and historically-contingent gesture.[73] In the meantime, pop-music artists have gone off in another direction, one that hardly affirms any theories as to the objecthood of noise. To the contrary; the examples I discuss below demonstrate that noise is now being used 1) to evoke a distinctly non-human subjectivity, and 2) to inspire pity for that subjectivity.

Pita (Peter Rehberg) is the founder of the electronica label Editions Mego. This detail is important because Mego released one of the more successful crossover glitch albums, Fennesz's *Endless Summer* (2001), which uses cascading walls of noise to subvert the breeziness of surf rock and beach culture. *Endless Summer* and the track I want to consider here, Track 3 from Pita's album *Get Out* (1999), are of a piece in that they both saturate an underlying melody with noise, not the noise of a scratched compact disc or vinyl record, but the acoustic surfeit of overloaded amplifiers. *Get Out* Track 3 uses a sample from Ennio Morricone's soundtrack for the Italian film *Come Maddelena* (1971). Pita begins the track by letting the unadulterated sample play briefly. There is a wordless female chorus intoning a modally-tinted melody that sounds like a choral anthem from one of Morricone's Spaghetti Western soundtracks. After this first straightforward iteration, noise floods the track, a deluge that all but overwhelms the Morricone theme for the next ten minutes. There are other examples of inundating a melody, whether sampled or arranged or newly composed, with phonographic noise: not only Fennesz's *Endless Summer*, but his earlier cover of the Rolling Stones' "Paint It Black" (1998), and of the New Orleans-based group Belong's work, particularly their cover of Syd Barrett's "Late Night" (2006). There is, of course, the famous example of William Basinski's *The Disintegration Loops* (2001), for which the decaying tape medium literally destroys the musical material it bears with each successive playback. The tradition could be traced even earlier to The Jesus and Mary Chain tracks such as "Just Like Honey" (1985). My earlier observations about this type of affect, a "negative beauty" that ultimately reinforces consonance by burying it in distortion, can well be valid.[74] But what now strikes me about this approach is less the aesthetic hierarchy it imposes than the ethical unease that it provokes. This is a different affect than that of, say, Debussy's "La cathédrale engloutie", where a submerged melody and the architecture it evokes rise up from the depths, resplendent and commanding. There is something pathetic in melodies that are distorted with phonographic noise. Pita leaves us with the impression that Morricone's theme *had* agency, but is now suffering. In such works, the melody undergoes an automatic process, and the artist can sympathize only through rendering that suffering into art.

Grouper (Liz Harris) is an electronica artist who works with her voice, synthesizers, and tape, as well as acoustic instruments. Her debut album, *Way Their Crept* (2005), builds from the precedent of Alvin Lucier's "I Am Sitting In A Room" and Steve Reich's "It's Gonna Rain", and it works wonderfully well. Harris' voice is always submerged in thick echoes as well as ambient reverberation, a regular, quick pulsation suffused with vaporous sound. Her voice is thus a shadow, at times indistinguishable from the accompanying instruments, at others, overdubbed onto itself. In the track "Close Cloak", this treatment divests Harris' voice of any capacity to communicate through lyrics; at times, it's not even clear whether there were lyrics to be heard. This phonographic surfeit denatures both Harris' voice and the whole of the album. It is clear that there must be some core to all this beautiful mess, some substrate to which the ambience can cling. And Harris' foggy melancholy exists because she has taken her voice – *her voice, her subjectivity* – and shorn it of agency. The voice is no longer Harris, and this is an agonizing thing to do to one's own self. It is now an amalgam of reverb and memory, forlorn and abject. In her 2011 album *Alien Observer*, the same techniques are set to work even more explicitly. In the title track, heavily reverberant broken guitar chords accompany Harris' several-times overdubbed voice. Lyrics are unintelligible except at the chorus, when they synchronize to intone, "Gonna take a spaceship, fly up to the stars / Alien observer of a world that isn't mine". This brief conjunction of vocal lines is rare in Grouper's work, and that it should coincide with lyrics that speak of an alien is significant. Grouper goes even further than Pita in expressing pity for the denatured melody, because melody here is always borne by the voice, the most intimate and subjective of instruments. Through noise and manipulation, Grouper transforms this subjectivity into a suffering, alienating presence.

I want to turn to hiphop artist Flume's track "Holdin On" (2012), which treats its sounds as pitiful, flesh-like, even horrific. "Holdin On" samples from Anthony White's 1977 Salsoul cover of Otis Redding's "I Can't Turn You Loose". The key motive of the track first occurs when White sings the two title words, starting at 0:01. White's pitch warbles on "holdin", even more so than in the original recording. Flume's treatment of the sample exaggerates the plaintiff urgency of the voice, which is indeed struggling to hold on to hope. The lyrics speak of a mad love, but their meaning is less important than how they are made to fall on the three chords in a ii-V-I progression, which itself is looped every eight bars. The repetition is inexorable and spasmodic. Unlike many hiphop productions from the 1990s, "Holdin On" makes no attempt to integrate its 1970s-era sample with the rest of the track.[75] The White sample is positioned in the center of the listener's stereophonic field, and it features no reverberation. But the female background singers sound distant, as if in a voluminous space, an acoustic discrepancy that underscores the impossibility of the track, the fact that it is constructed with sounds that would never inhabit the same field in real life. The constant repetition of a voice under duress calls attention to its status as material that is animated from without. And there are other indications of monstrosity. Like many tracks these days, "Holdin On" nods toward big-tent EDM by using the ascending glissando at the beginning of the track at 0:13, and again at 1:17. (This convention builds anticipation, and in many EDM tracks, immediately precedes the "drop" or moment when the percussion loudly accompanies the main melody of the track.) But Flume treats what could have remained a cliché quite literally. He subjects the background singers to an analogous pitch-raise starting at 1:53. This is an odd moment, when something taken for granted in a pop song is suddenly subverted to become freakish. If the conventions of a traditional soul song (such as that sung by Anthony White or Otis Redding) are that the singer communicates subjectivity through lyrics, expression, and lungs, here, that process has been stripped of its humanity. Flume's singer possesses a formerly organic voice that has been hooked up to an electric-shock machine. That voice still sings when current surges through it, but its song never changes, and always sounds out of place amid its acoustic surroundings. Sampling has been compared to necrophilia or grave-robbing,[76] but few instances of sampling are as uncanny as "Holdin On" in their crafting of samples as inert materials that are artificially brought to life.

Oneohtrix Point Never (Daniel Lopatin) also ruminates on the pathos of musical material. Like Flume, he flaunts the sutures that bind together the sounds of his track "Chrome Country" (2013). But OPN imposes a gauzy euphoria, starting with the vaporous opening chord progression (0:00–0:30) that provides the ostinato for the track. Starting at 0:30, we hear a truncated imitation of a panpipe, an electric piano playing neo-baroque figures (0:48), even a wordless children's chorus (1:16). OPN is somehow able to reconcile the technology of schlocky '80s pop (i.e. panpipes, fake kotos like in A Taste of Honey's "Sukiyaki") with the glitches of millennial gloom. At 4:05, a *deus ex machina*-moment of sorts occurs with the entrance of a church organ playing Alberti-bass figuration. The sutures are still audible, but somehow reconciled thanks to the patriarchal reimposition of order.

If the fiction at play is that the material of "Holdin On" and "Chrome Country" is vivisected living matter, what is the truth?

That artistic materials neither live nor suffer, that no living being is tortured by Flume or OPN. Sequencers, samplers, and digital audio-processing can carve up, reassemble, and mutate sound. But musical sound is neither alive nor non-human; it is as much a product of human labor, and thus an extension of humanity, as language or painting. Why then do we assume that we treat our artistic materials the way we treat one another? The fiction of a pitiful posthuman music draws on an ancient preoccupation of aesthetics. This preoccupation originates with Aristotle, whose *Poetics* describes the purifying properties of tragedy. Art can move us to pity by making us look at horrible events. Though we are not personally affected, we grieve as though we were. When the show is over, we emerge, cleansed and edified. Aristotle mentions how art *should* function, but recent history has forced the question of how art can also malfunction. Edmund Burke, for instance, notes that we experience not pity, but enjoyment, at watching aestheticized suffering of others.[77] And Paul Virilio argues that contemporary art reflects the bestial violence unleashed since World War I.[78] He regards artistic procedures like cubism, which fragments perspective, as perpetuations of violence. Virilio's critique is radical: we treat our artistic materials in ways similar to how we treat one another. Twentieth-century technologies for mass destruction have influenced technologies for sound treatment like the sampler and sequencer, which generate aesthetic materials by dismembering and reconstituting sound. Art must return to humanity by treating its materials and subject matter with pity.

Virilio's argument presents a certain compelling logic. It makes sense to suppose that we will enjoy cutting up people if we enjoy cutting up sounds, that artistic depictions of violence desensitize us to real violence. But historical practice and personal experience refute Virilio's position. We empathize with materials in pop, particularly those materials that seem to represent our subjectivity. Those subjective materials are, not surprisingly, those that seem most introspective: melody, lyrics, and the voice itself. We may cry when we hear a moving song, or enjoy singing along to karaoke. We do such things because we feel complicity with these elements of music.

So when popular music subjects those materials with which we feel the greatest sympathy to processes that deform sound, we feel not delight, but rather pity. For something has happened to melodies distorted by phonographic noise. My original interpretation, and that of other artists and writers, has been that noise is in an adversarial relationship with our subjectivity. Noise fights us, in other words. But the examples profiled here point to a different fiction: that the noisy material that suffers such trials is not just another recapitulation of us, the victorious human subjects who create and listen to it. That sound, that victimized sound, is no longer us.[79]

Change and Evolution

In early May 2015, news outlets such as Music.mic online magazine ran articles with headlines that ran like this: "Scientists Just Determined the Most Important Genre of Music of All Time".[80] The ensuing articles attempted to pick a fight between seniors, assumed to be parochial in their taste for the Beatles and Stones, and younger listeners, who presumably would be delighted that the study referred to late-1980s hiphop as the most revolutionary type of music in the last fifty years. The media reception implied a vindication of black music at the expense of white. The scientific article in question was indeed bold, but not for the reasons touted in the headlines. Its findings presented a version of pop-music history that, its authors bragged, was superior because of its reliance on "data". And this data supposedly demonstrated that popular music "evolves" in a manner analogous to biological organisms. The authors proclaimed that their contribution outpaced the theories of "philosophers, sociologists, bloggers and pop stars", which were inferior because they were steeped in "vivid musical lore and aesthetic judgments".[81] And although the article itself was reported with great éclat, its new methodology passed unnoticed. Without their even knowing it, musicologists' livelihoods were quietly called into question.

I single out this article, and related research by its two principal authors, not to defend musicology from extradisciplinary encroachments. The authors' techniques for extracting information from large pools of data are effective. When used in concert with historical and aesthetic research, these methods can enrich our understanding of the nature and tempo of stylistic change in pop. But the enthusiasm for interdisciplinary research and STEAM (science, technology, engineering, arts, and mathematics) in particular should not distract us from what are perennial obligations of scholarly research, no matter how old-fashioned that may sound. At play in this essay are semantic slippages and the consequences of not properly defining one's terms, both of research and engagement.

* *

The article in question, "The evolution of popular music: USA 1960-2010", appeared in the online journal *Royal Society Open Science* on 9 April 2015. Its two lead co-authors are Matthias Mauch, a music infomatics researcher at Queen Mary, University of London, and Robert M. MacCallum, a computational biologist at Imperial College, London. Mauch/MacCallum (2015) states at the outset that what distinguishes the study is its use of music informational retrieval (MIR), the study of methods for culling measurable information from music. MIR embraces a variety of techniques, one of which is the categorizing of salient features within large sample pools of musical works. The fact that so many recordings are now available online, in digital format, and cheaply or for no cost at all, has enabled researchers to expand the applications for MIR. Mauch/MacCallum (2015) uses MIR to answer the following questions: "has the variety of popular music increased or decreased over time? Is evolutionary change in popular music continuous or discontinuous? And, if it is discontinuous, when did the discontinuities occurs?"[82] The article sets out with this invocation of "evolutionary change", and later on, elides "change" with "evolution" as well as "revolution". Yet Mauch/MacCallum (2015) does not, in fact, state what is meant by "evolution", except implicitly when it refers to both "cultural and organismic variety" resulting from "modification-by-descent".[83] Otherwise, the stylistic changes Mauch/MacCallum (2015) measures pertain to the appearance and disappearance of timbral and emotive aspects, changes that are perceivable over the course of months and years. Mauch/MacCallum (2015) never mentions terms central to Darwinian evolutionary theory such as natural selection, artificial selection, survival of the fittest, or the struggle for existence.[84] But it does proffer a syllogism: "Just as paleontologists have discussed the tempo and mode of evolutionary change in the fossil record, historians of music have discussed musical change and the processes that drive it."[85] Although the two clauses are separately true, the "just as" would have us think that paleontologists and music historians' methodologies are comparable. Are they?

The absence of evolutionary theory in an article arguing for cultural evolution is striking, even if Mauch/MacCallum (2015) might retort that social scientists have already established that cultural evolution exists. What Mauch/MacCallum (2015) does succeed in providing, and quite admirably at that, is a quantifiable description of salient stylistic trends in a very particular subset of Anglo-American popular music spanning a fifty-year period. As the authors state, "These styles rise and fall in frequency over time in response to the changing tastes of songwriters, musicians and producers, who are in turn influenced by the audience".[86] But this characterization of stylistic change says nothing of the fact that, for much of the five-decade period in question, chart success had more to do with intrusions such as payola, advertising, and music-video publicity than it did with the supposedly disinterested taste of the consumer. The decision to pass over the music industry's influence on chart placement puts Mauch/MacCallum (2015) at some remove from the aims of Darwinian evolutionary theory, which explains species diversity as resulting from natural selection of characteristics that best enable an organism to adapt to its environment. If anything, Mauch/MacCallum (2015) might frame its argument as artificial selection, the practice whereby humans selectively breed specific organisms to produce desired stock.[87] As it stands, the article's sample pool is limited in the same way that many college courses on pop music are, through favoring the songs that enjoyed heavy rotation on radio stations from the 1960s through the 1990s. This homogeneous collection of tracks yields a set of musical characteristics that, while varied, nonetheless adhere to certain general trends. Traits like hooks, guitar or keyboard solos, verse-and-chorus form, break sections, and even the image and personae of the performing artists do not arise arbitrarily, as if through mutation. Natural selection does not, therefore, reinforce those traits most capable of producing hits. Rather, chart-topping musical characteristics arise as a result of a cocktail of influence and imitation, outright plagiarism, recording-studio chemistry, audience appreciation, and business speculation – all traits that evade MIR techniques or data acquisition in general, yet that merit historical and aesthetic analysis. Mauch/MacCallum (2015) thus commits the following methodological faults: 1) it applies evolutionary theory unevenly and selectively; 2) it asserts a syllogism between paleontology and musicology; and 3) it weighs only data acquired through digital analysis, largely discounting humanistic research.

In their previous article from 2012, MacCallum and Mauch set out to demonstrate the role of consumer choice on "music evolution".[88] And while Mauch/MacCallum (2015) invokes evolutionary theory only nominally, MacCallum/Mauch (2012) places it centrally in its methodology. The authors created a "Darwinian music engine" called "DarwinTunes", a computer program that generates "tree-like digital genomes" that themselves encode programs. Each program produces "a short, seamlessly looping polyphonic sound sequence" – a fragmented loop, in other words. These loops are "recombined" rather than being faithfully repeated through the introduction of "random genetic material", a sort of musical mutation. "Selection" occurs when participant-listeners rate the loops; those loops rated in the top half of their respective generation are allowed to continue (i.e. "survive") to the next generation, while those rated in the bottom half disappear (i.e. "go extinct"). The authors claim to demonstrate that listener choice initially contributes to the evolution of loops into what is clearly music, sounds having "aesthetically pleasing chords and rhythms". But then, evolution slows or even stops because "fidelity of transmission becomes an increasing impediment to progress as adaptation proceeds".[89] This slowing explains why "musical styles in premodern societies appear to be very conservative"[90] – "low transmission fidelity" results when musicians experiment and learn new techniques.

In comparison with Mauch/MacCallum (2015), MacCallum/Mauch (2012) explicitly applies evolution, going so far as to assert that DarwinTunes gives rise to species of musical organisms that "sexually reproduce and mutate".[91] This experiment supposedly demonstrates a type of selection dependent on listener feedback. But the argument reduces the creative process to the desire to cater to the likes and dislikes of listeners, which assumes a degree of listener power and interventional discernment that beggars belief. MacCallum/Mauch (2012) assumes a *Gong Show*-like process whereby music survives or perishes based on the whims of the audience. Both of Mauch's and MacCallum's articles pose metaphysical questions that also preoccupied the Frankfurt and Birmingham Schools: why are there many types of music rather than few or only one? Who determines what types of music there are? And while both articles admit the limits of their methodologies (the fact that MIR and DarwinTunes so far cannot account for compositional influences and industry forces), these pressures are waved away as secondary. In reality, the decision to treat music as an evolving organism means that we treat music as a commodity, infinitely responsive to the taste of the customer.

* *

This is not the first time that evolutionary theory has appeared alongside music. In *The Descent of Man* (1871), Darwin discusses birdsong as a tool of sexual selection, and infers that early instances of musical activity among primates may have served a similar function.[92] This acknowledgment on the part of Darwin of music's presence in human evolution is significant because of what Darwin mentions, but also what he does not. The ability and inclination to make music is an adaptation of hominids to their environment and to intra-species competition. But Darwin does not describe music itself as undergoing evolutionary change. Bennett Zon relates how enthusiasm for evolutionary theory took root in nineteenth-century English music scholarship. Here, the point of reference was less Darwin than his contemporary, Herbert Spencer, who promulgated the view that evolution was necessarily a progressive change from lesser to greater complexity. Victorian "musicology dispensed its knowledge and values in discernibly linear stories, and those stories – principally about composers and their compositions – relied upon development and recapitulation in a way that

Darwinian evolution could never satisfy".[93] Darwin himself would not have recognized his theory in such music discussions because he regarded evolution as adaptation to an organism's surroundings, not necessarily a development or improvement.[94] Yet for late nineteenth- and early twentieth-century music scholars, from Francis Heuffer to Heinrich Schenker, music history was a tree of life linking a progenitor (like Schubert) to the blossoming of a tradition (e.g. Wagner), and musical material itself (when masterfully deployed, as in Beethoven) contained within isolated motifs and chords the kernel for organic development.[95] It is hardly new, in other words, to rationalize music in evolutionary terms, even if those terms are not Darwinian.

The approaches outlined above – to frame music within the evolutionary change of hominids, and to make sense of stylistic change as progress – have gained momentum since the Victorian era to comprise disciplines of their own. Evolutionary musicology starts its watch with Darwin's observations on birdsong and sexual selection, and drawing on evidence from archaeology and paleontology, charts the chain of events that led to musical behaviors in animals, including *homo sapiens*. But this project has an obvious pitfall: how to discern biological change from cultural change. The temptation might be to single out biological change from habits, practices, customs, and behaviors. But Tomlinson's recent book advocates for a "coevolution" stance that conceives of both social and biological evolution as occurring incrementally and in concert. As Tomlinson puts it, these two dynamics feed one another: "We must think not only of avian biology shaping birdsong, but also of birdsong cultures shaping biology."[96] The fiction in this newest attempt to link evolution with music is not that the British Invasion wasn't a peak of innovation, nor that stylistic diversity is either on the decline or on the ascent. Rather, it is one of disciplines and semantics: that cultural evolution more or less operates like biological evolution, and that change is evolution. It will come as no surprise that musicology has had some difficulty shaking its own bias toward progressive narratives. The idea that Western composition was inherently superior to non-Western music drew on the competing brand of evolutionary theory prevalent in the Victorian era, Herbert Spencer's teleology, which held that all species evolved from lesser to greater complexity. That progression supposedly culminated with mankind. Spencerian evolutionary theory informed the work of musicologists like Guido Adler, but the narrative of incremental betterment was already commonplace thanks to Hegel's theory of the inevitable progress of history. The study of popular music, itself a much younger field born amid discussions of postmodernity, has made some attempts to divest itself of progressive histories. But these are stubborn fixations, abetted by the music industry's own mechanisms (like corporate radio stations devoted to "Classic Rock") for canon formation. Mauch/MacCallum (2015) relies on a fuzzy conception of evolution that borrows terminology from Darwinian theory, rationalizes itself as an extension of cultural-evolutionary theory, and yet is neither.

The field of cultural evolution has presented compelling theories explaining, for instance, why certain words in a given language fall out of usage.[97] Any cultural practice, whether the transmission of a language, or construction of a tool, or stylistic change in a form of music or other art, displays three character-istics taken directly from Darwin: variation, competition, and inheritance.[98] Variation is undeniably present in Mauch and MacCallum's sample pool. But competition and inheritance are less easily quantified. Reducing competition to chart success is reductive, even when considering a commercial artform like pop. Tracks that sell well aren't necessarily influential, just as influ-ential tracks don't necessarily sell well; just recall the Velvet Underground, virtually unknown during their brief existence, now dubbed "the most important band that no one heard" because of their delayed significance to punk, postpunk, and

1990s folk-rock. Inheritance is an even cagier quality, for influence can be gauged specifically on the basis of particular sounds or moments, or generally, as when we observe one style growing out of another. These two terms work well in a Darwinian context, but success in biology is relatively easy to define. The organism that is able to adapt to its environment long enough to reproduce has succeeded, according to the terms of evolution. Whether those adaptions are great or small in scale is immaterial, so long as survival of the species is the result.

Without using the word "evolution", Mauch/MacCallum (2015) could have stated that change in pop-music styles has been more or less constant between 1960 and 2010, with the years 1964, 1983, and 1991 witnessing unusually brisk stylistic change. Contrary to anecdotal evidence of the paucity of contemporary music, stylistic diversity has not diminished since 1960. Similarly, MacCallum/Mauch (2012) could have explained DarwinTunes as an attempt to measure the effect of listener input on stylistic diversity, all the while acknowledging that "listener input", as solicited in the experiment, bears little resemblance to the ways in which listeners actually influence musical creativity. In both articles, the authors could have stated that "pop music", far from being an ideologically neutral entity, is a product of preferential practices that make comparisons to biological organisms, or even other cultural phenomena, tricky at best. As it stands, the phenomena measured in the two papers establish only one of the three conditions for evolution: variation.

The elision between stylistic change and progress, and from progress onto evolution, is a difficult habit to kick for researchers as well as musicians and listeners. Evolution is engrained in the very sounds upon which pop music relies. Listen to Daft Punk's "Giorgio By Moroder" (2013). The track combines Moroder's own commentary on his career with variations on a dance theme. It's an infectious track: Moroder begins by describing his first years as a DJ for a German discothèque in the early 1970s, when he was only sixteen years old. The theme first appears as soft soul, then picks up the tempo to become lean, understated disco. Moroder then says that he initially "wanted to do an album with the sounds of the 50s, the sounds of the 60s, the sounds of the 70s, and then, a sound of the future", the latter of which drew him towards what has since become his signature style, synthesized mechanized figuration beneath soaring, coldly beautiful melodies. After introducing himself ("My name is Giovanni Giorgio, but everybody calls me Giorgio"), Moroder's voice drops out, and the theme assumes this futuristic form for a few repetitions before changing to Latin jazz, then back to Moroder's posthuman landscape. When Moroder's voiceover returns, he speaks of freeing "your mind of the concept of harmony and of music being correct". The music then abruptly changes to acoustic strings, in classical style for sixteen bars. Then, a drum set enters, fusing rock with classical and Moroder's future-past synthesizers, and the sum total resembles today's big-room house style. Of course, all of this music is being produced by Daft Punk, a duo devoted to amalgams of 1970s disco, 1980s electronica, and house of the 1990s. It's a classy homage to one of their inspirations (and with its descending glissando disintegrating into discrete clicks of noise, it ends with another homage, this time to Stockhausen's *Kontakte*). Although Moroder never uses the word "evolution" here, the piece sets up a progression from disco to "the sound of the future". It's a celebration of where electronic music came from, and where it can go in the future.

Or, at least that's how Daft Punk intends the track. In "Giorgio By Moroder", change is progress, and evolution goes hand-in-hand with honoring the past. But in the commercial music industry in which competition is so difficult do define ("unsuccessful" pop music doesn't disappear from circulation, after all), where no recording dies, and where inheritance follows no logic, the only remaining marker of evolution is variation. The most striking change since 2000 has been that the period of recycling seems to be decreasing; whereas the cycle for revivals used to be about twenty years (e.g. the disco revival of the 1990s), revivals today rehash styles current only ten or five or even two years previously. Simon Reynolds regards "Giorgio By Moroder" as conscious recycling of the past, without what used to be a concomitant desire to innovate.[99] Moroder himself tells us that, as a young man, he wanted to make "a sound of the future". And Daft Punk's (admittedly wonderful) response to this once-imagined future is to project its own fantasmic future, a sound that blends string sounds of the classical style with rock percussion and Daft Punk's own retrohouse style of the early 2000s. "Giorgio By Moroder" is in fact that most regressive of forms, theme-and-variations, and its variations lead not to a sound of the future, but to the past.

Any investigative methodology, whether scientific or speculative, detects best that which it was intended to measure. The MIR methods mentioned here constitute a watershed in our ability to perceive trends and patterns in large quantities of recordings. But in limiting the sample pool to charting songs, we ignore the massive ocean of music that was never commercially competitive with pop hits, and yet bequeathed a formidable inheritance to future artists.

Style Is Intellectual Property

The fiction considered above envisions that musical style changes according to the principles of cultural evolution, and Mauch and MacCallum make a stronger (if methodologically problematic) claim that this change occurs according to the principles of biological evolution. The fiction to which I want to turn now builds on a related claim: that change in pop style occurs in a way that is comparable to the way genetic mutations introduce divergence within a species. The purpose of this claim is to assert that musical style is intellectual property. The material specificity of this fiction, with its broad legal and aesthetic implications, distinguishes it from the weaker claim that music merely evolves. For this fiction deploys a rhetoric that traces musical characteristics across time, as transferred between artists and styles. This musical genealogy mirrors the field of phylogenetics, which studies evolution through the inheritance of physical and genetic traits. This radical reconceptualization forces pop musicians and listeners to confront dilemmas new to music discourse, but that are also present in bioethics: what defines an individual, whether that individual is an organism or a musical work? What defines a species, and what defines a musical style? And what in an individual's genetic makeup should be patentable, just as what about a musical work should be copyrightable? In short, we can sum up this fiction as the idea that a musical style can count as an intellectual property.

To begin, contemplate the statement by geneticist Adam Rutherford, that pop genres such as rock and hiphop arose thanks to "imperfect copying", just as genetic mutations do.[100] This is not a gratuitous analogy, and would certainly not seem to be a thought-fiction. Rutherford likens remixing and sampling to what happens to genes at the moment of fertilization, when the genetic sequences of egg and sperm are copied and combine to form the DNA for a new organism. Such copies are for the most part faithful, but a certain amount of divergence or mutation is inevitable in every offspring. This divergence introduces variation to the gene pool, and variation, recall from above, is one of Darwin's three criteria for evolution. Mutation, in other words, is requisite for evolution. Similarly, hiphop's sampling of funk and R&B copied a tradition but introduced variations in the form of newly composed rap lyrics and layering of beats and samples. Hiphop thus contains material traces of its antecedents, just as the DNA of any organism contains genetic traces of its ancestors. As expressed by Rutherford, this concept exists as a helpful analogy, but not a thought-fiction, for Rutherford certainly is not advocating belief in something he knows is not true. The fiction of style's intellectual-property status arises more or less independently of scientific discussion, but with the result that litigious producers and owners treat musical artifacts as pharmaceutical companies treat genes and genetically related species. This fiction is thus a series of small steps that, when taken as a whole, indicate a stark digression from earlier values of property and metaphysics.

Before we can contemplate the phylogenetic turn of pop-music discourse, we need to evaluate the state of pop-music retromania as reflected in the strange rise of the "new sound-alike". Let's begin with Glass Candy's "Digital Versicolor" (2007), a faultless specimen of the style of Giorgio Moroder. Its repeated sixteenth-notes, treated to a judicious amount of modulation, recall Moroder's soundtrack for the 1978 film *Midnight Express*. Its female vocal line, too ethereal for most 1970s-era disco, instead derives from Donna Summer's "I Feel Love" (1977), the track that Moroder famously produced. And the climactic entrance of "Digital Versicolor"'s operatic synth melody, an entrance that takes nearly four minutes to arrive, recalls the Italo Disco abjection of Moroder's soundtrack for the 1980 film *American Gigolo*. "Digital Versicolor" is not an ironic invocation of Moroder's music. One might argue that it is not even a revival, for revivalism supposes a belief that a style is dead but can be momentarily resuscitated. Glass Candy operates as if Moroder's style were as current today as it was in its heyday, a sort of retromania in denial. "Digital Versicolor" exhibits a type of retromania I'll dub the "new sound-alike", meaning a work that emulates the style of one or multiple works. In the new sound-alike, no material is copied and thus no copyright is infringed; this distinguishes it from other forms of musical appropriation like sampling or covering. We can thus observe that "Digital Versicolor", for instance, emulates Moroder's style without lifting any melodies of Moroder's compositions. And yet we know this to be in the style of Moroder, not Philly soul or David Bowie or Kraftwerk.

The worst of the era of sampling lawsuits is, for all intents and purposes, over. In its wake, the new sound-alike has assumed a prominent position among today's pop musicians. Instead of stealing musical objects from the past, artists create semblances of the past, and these semblances are perfectly legal. If we investigate how these semblances are constructed, we can understand their function as both intellectual property and as ontological objects. The new sound-alike requires us to reconsider the dimensions of the musical work. Applications of copyright law prior to 2015 suggested that the essence of a musical composition resided in its melody (and lyrics, if present). The secondary characteristics of the musical work were supposedly incidental qualities like harmony, rhythm, and timbre – aesthetically important to be sure, but possessing no property status. But the new sound-alike has uprooted prior notions of essence and secondary characteristics. Music copyright is now being applied in a manner similar to the way that patent law is being applied to DNA.

The history of music copyright is a tale of two forms of musical creativity: the composition and the sound recording. To summarize briefly a chronology that has been documented elsewhere[101], the 1909 Copyright Act afforded to the burgeoning technology of phonography a regulated flexibility: the compulsory license that required publishers to authorize performances on the part of any musician (not only those chosen by the publisher), but only on the condition that a statutory licensing fee was paid to the publisher. This act ensured that publishers would be compensated not only for sheet-music reproductions and live performances, but also for mechanized renditions realized with piano rolls. It also set the stage for the "cover song" to play an integral role in the subsequent rise of mass commercial pop.

A cover is a performance of a track by someone other than its original performer. It was not a new practice in 1909, of course, but it accrued particular significance with the development of American pop-music forms in the 1950s such as rhythm and blues and its famous younger sibling, rock and roll. Cover songs typically entail a more or less faithful reperformance of a melody, even if the original's rhythm, tempo, or instrumentation are altered. The expansion of commercial radio combined with the slow movement toward racial desegregation meant that styles associated with either black or white listeners began to share both stylistic characteristics and audiences. The 1909 Act made it possible for cover songs to be profitable for publishers. Cover licenses reinforced the primacy of melody and lyrics as property, and also normalized the notion that style, the quotient of those musical characteristics *other than* melody and lyrics, was generally available for public use and did not, therefore, qualify for copyright.

Even today's Copyright Code is terse on what in a musical composition qualifies for protection: "Copyright protection subsists, in accordance with this title, in original works of authorship fixed in any tangible medium of expression [...] Works of authorship include [...] musical works, including any accompanying works."[102] The Code gives no other clarification as to which parts of a musical work might be protected; indeed, it does not even mention specific musical phenomena such as "melody", "harmony", and "rhythm". But in legal decisions over the last century, "uncopyrightable elements [...] generally include a song's theme [i.e. subject matter of lyrics], individual words, individual notes, short musical phrases, rhythm, and harmony".[103] A harmony on its own rarely qualifies for copyright, although it "can certainly contribute to the copyrightability of a musical composition as a whole".[104] And because many pop songs have a similar 4/4 meter, "rhythm alone will rarely be sufficiently original to merit copyright protection".[105] In practice, rhythm and harmony can buttress claims for a passage's copyrightability, but only insofar as they are paired with a unique melody.

If we apply traditional intellectual-property parlance to the constituent parts of the musical composition, we might say that melody and lyrics have, for the twentieth and the beginning of the twenty-first centuries, been received as the expressions of the idea of an original work. And while ideas are not eligible for protection under copyright, expressions of ideas are.[106] Compare the porousness of the composition copyright to the copyright for sound recordings, which (even before they were included for protection under federal statue in 1971) treated *all* sounds, whether melodic, lyric, or otherwise, as protectable.[107] Thus, in a copyrighted recording of a song with an extensive percussion break – in, say, Michael Viner's Incredible Bongo Band's "Apache" (1973) – the sound of that break is protected even though its rhythm, as it exists as a separate composition, is not.

The rise of commercial popular music since the mid-1950s helped recordings surpass compositions in terms of aesthetic and financial value. And because the sound-recording copyright emerged after, and is distinct from, the copyright for compositions, the scope of the sound-recording copyright is more inclusive than that for compositions. Hiphop popularized sampling or appropriating pre-existing recordings as an artistic practice. From the beginning of the hiphop movement in the late 1970s through the early 1990s, most samples were acquired without permission from labels or original recording artists, which led to a number of high-profile lawsuits.[108] Of these suits, the definitive statement on unauthorized sampling is still the Sixth Circuit's 2005 decision in *Bridgeport vs. Dimension*.[109] Bridgeport Music published many of George Clinton's hits, and in 1983, Clinton signed over the rights to many of his recordings to the publisher in order to repay a million-dollar advance. Since 1991, Bridgeport has capitalized on this catalog by filing lawsuits against approximately 800 record labels it accused of illegally sampling Parliament and Funkadelic songs.[110] In its case against

Dimension Films, Bridgeport accused the rap group N.W.A of illegally sampling its recording of Funkadelic's "Get Off Your Ass and Jam". A Tennessee District Court had previously ruled that the sample, a repeated, three-note, electric-guitar arpeggio, was a *de minimis* sample requiring no clearance.[111] Sixth Circuit Judge Ralph Guy reversed this decision, declaring: "A sound recording owner has the exclusive right to 'sample' his own recording [...] Get a license or do not sample."[112] Guy's opinion delineates music compositions from sound recordings. Music compositions are creative material for which copyright provides substantial but not absolute protection, because a thriving musical culture allows musicians to reference (but not copy) the work of others liberally. But sound recordings, Judge Guy states, are physical products whose monetary value suffers when even small portions from them are duplicated.[113] To invoke the idea/expression divide mentioned above, the "composition" as it exists in printed form is provisional because it exists only as indications for how to make music sound. The composition has therefore assumed a more abstract status in comparison to the concrete, sometimes tangible phenomenon of the sound recording. Although copyright scholars would object to my wording, compositions have, until 2015, been treated more as ideas rather than as expressions, whereas, thanks to the *Bridgeport* decision, recordings are the ultimate protectable expression.

The permissive composition copyright has called forth the new sound-alike, a form of stylistic emulation as close to plagiarism as one can legally dare. Such new sound-alikes have assumed a prominent role in popular music of the last twenty years. To take just one example: consider the responses to Track IV from Jean-Michel Jarre's 1976 album *Oxygène*. Vangelis' acclaimed soundtrack for Ridley Scott's 1982 film *Blade Runner* features a track over the closing credits that displays marked similarities. Jarre's 12/8 triplets become Vangelis' 4/4-sixteenths, and both have waxing and waning swaths of chords. French EDM artist Vitalic created his own ode to Jarre's track with his 2005 recording, "The Past". And Oneohtrix Point Never's 2007 track "Betrayed In The Octagon" is a moody recreation of sci-fi soundtracks and futuristic horror. This sort of similarity, whether we call it "homage" or "theft" or "stylistic appropriation", has become a norm thanks in part to the constraints of the 2005 *Bridgeport* appeal ruling. For this reason, the release of Robin Thicke and Pharrell Williams' 2013 hit "Blurred Lines" wasn't especially surprising, for here was another song deliberately modeled on an earlier hit, Marvin Gaye's "Got To Give It Up" (1977). Thicke and Williams filed suit against the Gaye estate after Gaye's children publically commented on the similarity between the two tracks. The Gayes countersued, and a jury in March 2015 awarded $7.4 million in damages and composition writing credits to the Gaye estate.

It is easy to sympathize with the jury's rebuke of Williams and Thicke. It did not help that Thicke, publicly arrogant, clownish, and white, was lifting his song form a deceased, beloved, black icon of soul. And the swagger of Thicke and Williams, who readily admitted to copying the "feel" of Gaye's song, was breathtaking.[114] Nonetheless, the "Blurred Lines" decision threatens to criminalize songs that refer to past performers and styles. Unless checked by other legal decisions, *Williams v. Bridgeport* sweeps away the regulated flexibility of the composition copyright by bestowing property status on phenomena that were previously regarded as fleeting. A melody, an ensemble's instrumentation, a bassline, a singer's timbre – if enough of these are demonstrably taken from earlier works, a plaintiff now stands a chance of demonstrating infringement.

The composition copyright's compulsory license developed at the beginning of the era of commercial phonography. So it is not surprising that the values of the composition copyright reflect those of the era immediately prior to the phonographic era. What counted in late-nineteenth-century popular music were lyrics and melodies. Rhythms and instrumentation were not considered proprietary because they were frequently adapted according to the arrangement. Phonography changed this by rendering any recorded arrangement into something permanent. And sampling and sound-treatment technologies that have taken root since the 1980s have perpetuated this change by rending isolated sounds (that would previously have been deemed too transitory or trivial to count as property) into artistic materials in their own right. There are no longer distinctions between essence and accident thanks to the "Blurred Lines" ruling, because all attributes are now equally essential.

This leaves us in an interesting predicament in terms of the definition of style. It used to be that style in pop music was a general grouping into which similar tracks could fit. But those similarities were predicated on the accidental (meaning that which could be otherwise), rather than essential, qualities other than melody and lyrics. To draw a parallel to evolutionary genetics, the term "style" used to be analogous to "species", for the two connote (or until recently, used to connote) groups of similar entities. A species has traditionally been defined as a group of organisms that share the capacity for biparental sexual reproduction[115]; a style has traditionally referred to a recurring set of characteristics within an artistic work. Now, some evolutionary biologists are challenging the definition of "species", with some questioning the utility of the term, and others arguing that a species is an individual rather than a group. Similarly, style is being treated as a defining primary characteristic of a musical work, a characteristic deserving of intellectual-property protection. New sound-alikes demonstrate that style has now replaced melody as the defining attribute of a pop track. There is no longer any accidental background in music, whether in an aesthetic or legal sense. And with current technologies that allow musicians with little to no prior experience to create or borrow any imaginable sound, it is now possible to make music that sounds like any other type of music from any period. Indeed, the standard production method for the hit-driven music industry makes stylistic redundancy unavoidable. John Seabrook describes this as the track-and-hook approach, in which the different elements of a song are farmed out to different songwriters and lyricists:

> As a working method, track-and-hook tends to make songs sound the same. Dance music producers have always borrowed liberally from others' grooves. There's no reason not to: beats and chord progressions can't be protected under the existing copyright laws, which recognize only the melody and lyrics. [Seabrook wrote this before the "Blurred Lines" verdict.] As dance beats have become the backing tracks to a growing number of pop songs, similar-sounding records have proliferated.[116]

These technical and practical details make it so that it has never been easier to imitate preexisting styles. That, combined with the ubiquity of web-based applications like YouTube and Spotify, means that musicians today can learn and assimilate any style. Whereas in previous decades artists had to work simply to approximate a given sound, many artists today place great weight on the ability to emulate and perfect a style.

But what do we mean by "style", actually? In popular music, the term can refer to units of varying size, whether sounds within a track, the track itself, a single artist, a group of artists, an era, or a genre. Genre is vexingly close to style, signifying groupings of tracks that share definitive musical characteristics. Thus, "rock", "metal", "techno", "country", "hiphop", and "soul" are all genres, but could be described as styles, too. Allan F. Moore clarifies this muddle somewhat in stating that style is the "how" of music, meaning the technical traits, while genre is the "what" and "whence", meaning the traits that are socially constrained.[117] Conventional histories of popular music tend to emphasize the stability or predictability of styles. Hiphop artists, for instance, tend to remain hiphop artists; they do not migrate to emo or folk music. And hiphop, at least until the 2000s, could be counted on to feature a predictable set of traits: looped rhythms derived from funk or soul; samples; rapping, etc. But even as far back as the 1960s, there were inklings of the stylistic potpourri that has become today's status quo. In 1968, The Beatles released their eponymous *The Beatles* album, better known as *The White Album*, which as Reynolds points out is curio cabinet of pop styles and genres, from Beach Boys-like vocal harmonies ("Back In The USSR") and psychedelia ("Dear Prudence) to music hall ("Martha My Dear"), proto metal ("Helter Skelter"), and the avant-garde ("Revolution 9").[118] David Bowie in 1975 released his *Young Americans* album, which stands today as the most drastic left turn in a career fairly flush with them. (I'll speak more about Bowie and style in Part III.) If *The White Album* and Bowie were initially exceptions in an environment where styles otherwise remained consistent, shedding genres and styles as easily as costumes has since become a mainstream practice. Here are just a few recent examples:

1) Taylor Swift, who had previously garnered acclaim as a country artist, released in 2014 the album *1989*, a work Swift describes as her first "pop" album. Although Swift explains the album title as a nod to 1980s artists like Madonna and Annie Lennox, *1989*'s tracks are both an ode to pop from thirty years ago as well as a guide to mainstream contemporary pop. All the trademarks of mid-2010s production are there: auto-tune, potpourri assemblages of hints of genres (go-go, hiphop, Nu Soul, etc.). Swift's album takes the intriguing tack of parrying the very nostalgia that its title would seem to conjure. It is a work

about past style, but in which that style is noticeably absent.

2) Swedish EDM artist Avicii in 2013 released the track "Wake Me Up", which combines elements of progressive house and country. I was teaching a course on EDM shortly after this track was released. Those of my students who had already heard it were generally quite enthusiastic about the track. Those who hadn't already listened to it reacted more or less the same way that I did, with bemusement and some distaste. EDM and country do not, or at least did not before 2013, suggest a fruitful coupling, but robust sales around the world have since made "Wake Me Up" one of the most successful tracks of the decade. The economy with which the track evokes its two constituent styles distinguishes "Wake Me Up". We know that the track is progressive house on the basis of its tempo, its filtered build-ups and drop, and its fist-pumping refrain and beat. But "Wake Me Up" also contains an acoustic-guitar riff and a twangy male vocal line (provided by Aloe Blacc). "Wake Me Up" doesn't spend excessive time exploring the finer points of either house or country. These few traits are enough to broadcast genre without drowning us in it.

3) One could pick any number of Kanye West tracks to demonstrate how he experiments with style. I pick "Runaway" (2010) on the merits of its accompanying "full-length film", a thirty-four-minute surrealist parable likening West's creative genius to a beautiful woman wearing a bird costume. The length of this video allows West to touch on the genres for which he is best known: hiphop, of course, but also gospel and singer-songwriter ballads. "Runaway" also features extensive passages of Western classical orchestration. It is thus as exemplary of West's corpus as any of his tracks: an intuitive pastiche of styles that, unlike earlier hiphop sampladelia, seems

genuinely to love the genres that it deploys (rather than using them for shock value).

Much of the best popular music of the 1980s, 1990s, and 2000s featured sampling, and the technique is still prevalent. But samples used to be brief, and used to come from specific recordings. Now, the sampling is not of particular recordings, but rather styles and genres. This in itself is not a particularly revelatory observation. What is new is that these ubiquitous stylistic exchanges have led to the legal disputes that force an excessive reliance on musical phylogeny, and also threaten the very future of such exchanges.

Phylogeny in biology is the study of evolutionary ties between organisms. A tool frequently deployed here is the phylogenetic tree, a graphic representation of the relationships between organisms. Phylogenetic trees can indicate a "clade", which includes common ancestors and their descendants as well as the relative degree of divergence between progeny. Music researcher Gottfried Toussaint applies phylogenetic principles to the study of musical parameters. This methodology can, for instance, demonstrate concrete affinities between rhythmic patterns in African music, and such affinities can then be used to flesh out a picture of the evolution of such patterns.[119] Phylogenetic trees are fairly common as well in depictions of various EDM genres, which locate the ancestry of any contemporary subgenre in prior generations of disco and post-disco underground musics.[120] But notice that such phylogenetic analyses in music assume the existence of groups of individual songs; we could call these groups "genres" or "styles", or perhaps some other term, but the implication is clear that descent is predicated on one group drawing materials from another group.

What is different about the post-"Blurred Lines" world is that it has rendered style into an individual rather than a grouping. Style used to be considered a body of shared affinities, an abstract idea from which concrete, protectable expressions were derived. Style, in other words, used to be the provenance of the commons. The implication of the "Blurred Lines" ruling is that the style of a previously existing work (like "Got To Give It Up"), or even the style of a group of previously existing works (say, blues songs or soul songs), could be treated as individuals rather than groups or types. While this may sound at first like a purely semantic distinction, it means that we have arrived at more or less the same conclusion as evolutionary biologist Michael T. Ghiselin, who argues that species are individuals rather than types of individuals.[121] Individuals are expressions of ideas, and according to the foundation of copyright, can receive copyright protection. Moreover, the "Blurred Lines" verdict places us in similar territory to that of the intellectual-property status of genes. In 2013, the US Supreme Court ruled that naturally occurring genetic sequences are ineligible for patents.[122] At first glance, this decision would seem to affirm that "[l]aws of nature, natural phenomena, and abstract ideas are not patentable".[123] However, the decision goes on to state that synthetic departures from naturally occurring DNA can be patented: "the patent eligibility of a given cDNA molecule will depend on whether its sequence matches that of a naturally occurring DNA or, alternatively, reflects the removal of an intronic sequence."[124] This decision sets a low threshold for what constitutes synthetic DNA, just as the "Blurred Lines" decision sets a low threshold for what constitutes original, copyrightable expression in a musical composition. The fiction in this variant of musical phylogeny is that history and influence are no longer consequential, that all musical works are individuals only. This is outrageous fortune given that researchers intend for musical phylogeny to add to our understanding of music history, not detract from or compete with it. The legal application of musical phylogeny ends up repudiating the broadened perspective that phylogeny is supposed to bring. All tracks, and all parts of all tracks, are now commodities.

No future, indeed.

* *

We are sober twenty-first-century global citizens. We choose science over dogma, and celebrate the arts as emissaries for culture. Our appreciation of music and art is inflected by this utilitarian pragmatism. We will never again fall prey to ideology, whether in aesthetics or politics. So reads our alibi that absolves us of any embarrassment at contemplating, even if momentarily, the possibility that music could be alive. And yet, as the fictions above related, we tell ourselves many little lies about music's representation of subjectivity, of its stylistic evolution, of its eternal singularity. How are both positions possible?

Hegel would respond that we aren't lying to ourselves with these fictions. His system, which many might regard as itself a though-fiction, holds that "spirit" pervades objects both living and non-living, as well as human institutions like history, economics, and art. While Hegel did not believe that artworks were literally alive, he countered that artworks possessed something more vibrant and organic than living matter: the capacity to embody spirit in an enduring manner.[125] Meanwhile, if pressed about their claims of their research, Mauch and McCallum might well engage in some Lacanian disavowal about the nature of pop-music evolution – that they are not claiming to prove the existence of biological evolution, but rather a cultural evolution. Marx in turn might claim that biological fictions are another form of fetishism, of imbuing objects with no essential exchange value with the allure of living matter.

Negarestani provides an updated explanation of how rationalism and fiction can coexist in his mad novel *Cyclonopedia*. Characters separated by geography and culture and chronology share one belief, that oil, or the Middle East, or war are living entities:

Once settled, Um al-Ghathra began to write a treatise on what would later be called the Middle East as a sentient and living entity – alive in a very literal sense of the word, apart from all metaphor or allegory.[126]

After his last sermon, West started to search for a way to grasp war as an autonomous entity (to grasp war as a machine with machinic particles and parts).[127]

The dread in *Cyclonopedia* is that the dread of such horrific thoughts – that oil could be a living, sinister presence! – will overtake reason. The thought of the horror is more horrible than the horror itself. This situation is a corrective of the calm denial that Lacan identifies in his description of the role of a chorus in Greek tragedy, in which we defer belief in catharsis to the chorus. With the fictions associated with music's evolution, we might officially claim that music is not, could not be alive, and yet we simultaneously entertain tiny thought-fictions that could well inspire disquiet if faced head-on. That disquiet manifests itself through a nagging doubt, that music's vitality is temporary, provisional, weak. The fiction of music's life leads seamlessly to the fiction that music is dying out.

Part III

Music Is Dying Out

It has been the best of times and the worst of times, for those in the pop-music industry as for the rest of us. Never in history has so much music, in printed and recorded form as well as in live performance, been available for immediate and often free consumption. We drown in whirlpools of choice, of genre and format, mood and use. The rate of musical change seems, at least to some of those profiled in Part II, to be accelerating. And yet this abundance and speed and bounty is choking us. John Seabrook's 2015 exposé on the factory-production methods of the pop industry noted that "Radiohead's Thom Yorke memorably called Spotify 'the last desperate fart of a dying corpse...'"[128] Aside from the normal complaints of middle-aged listeners mourning the music of their youth, there exists an additional sense, shared by young and old, that something about pop is dying out.

If my previous discussion of musical phylogeny has succeeded in its goal, then it should have demonstrated that style has assumed other functions in contemporary pop. Every aspect of a given work is now regarded as essential, at least from legal and ethical standpoints. This means that the elements once viewed as accidental – *that which could be otherwise without changing the work's essence* – are now central. Style is no longer style; it is now substance, essence. Part III considers how discourses of stylistic regression cause us to conceptualize pop music as vulnerable to extinction. Because of the drastic changes in how music is produced, distributed, consumed, and sold, we have embraced a view that pop is an endangered species. The deaths of pop superstars such as David Bowie and Prince have only accentuated this sense of demise. Some react to this faith in imminent extinction by positing other worlds or fantastical realities ("A Society for Creative Anachronism"), or by creating new genres posited on the obsolescence of old ones ("Post-Genres"), or by engaging in "Acquisitive Philanthropy", the belief that listeners who choose to pay for music become patrons of the arts. These reflections invert the thesis in Part II, where I explored the thought-fiction that music is evolving. Here, we investigate thought-fictions asserting that pop music is dying out, or approaching extinction.

What We Lost in Losing Bowie

David Bowie died on 10 January 2016. Even now, it strikes me as absurd to write that Bowie could have died at all, let alone on a mundane, specific day, like any other mortal. I took the news hard, which was embarrassing given that I never met the man and had no personal connection with him other than through loving his music. But what was surprising to me in the coming days was the realization that I was far from alone. Judging by media coverage and word of mouth, most people above the age of thirty felt as if they had just lost an uncle, someone whose music was present during parties and adolescent milestones and in otherwise trivial memories. At the age of seven, I began watching MTV soon after the network was launched, and I fell for the charms of Bowie's platinum-blonde pompadour wig of the *Let's Dance* period, his chiseled, metallic-cheeked face in the "Blue Jean" video, even his garish yellow jumpsuit in the video for "Dancing In The Streets" with Mick Jagger. Some of my friends admitted that they hardly could conceive of life in which Bowie was not a reliable, if distant, point of reference. As one of them put it, "I hardly think it's possible for anything to kill the musician who made [album] *Scary Monsters*, but good try, cancer!"

Media tributes to Bowie said what one might have expected.

Many referred to Bowie as a chameleon who changed his persona and musical style multiple times. Those hoping to convey his importance to younger listeners wrote that Madonna and Lady Gaga would be incomprehensible or just plain impossible without Bowie, and here too, his stylistic promiscuity was front and center. Lady Gaga responded in kind by wearing *Aladdin Sane*-style face paint (with the lightning bolt) at the Grammy Awards on 15 February 2016, and a group of Belgian astronomers named a constellation after Bowie.[129] The word "icon" was bandied about as usual, and stars and civilians alike remembered Bowie for having the courage to be bisexual and to campaign for greater visibility for black artists on MTV, long before it was politically easy or profitable to do so. These were all sincere expressions of gratitude, and under other circumstances, would have been the sort of uplifting statement that would leave more sweetness than bitterness in the mouth.

But circumstances were what they were, and it was Bowie whom we lost, not some other celebrity. Such tributes bring me no comfort, and even today, I feel a type of loss that is strange and uncomfortable because it seems inappropriate to feel in such a manner about a celebrity. All the tributes and portraits, kind and deserved though they may be, don't explain this vague mourning, and thus offer me no comfort. Journalists and critics and university professors emphasize Bowie's stylistic transformations, but they overlook that Bowie himself remained latent, present in each manifestation. In our haste to talk about all his changes, we neglect that which stayed the same, from his first to last album.

That consistency is difficult to verbalize. Let's begin then with a tidbit from Bowie's formation: he was trained as a mime before he began his career as a pop musician. Miming may seem the antithesis of the rock and soul circles Bowie would later frequent, but what's important here is less some topical affinity between miming and music than the fact that a good mime can take up

73

and discard personas with a paradoxical combination of investment and detachment. Bowie as Ziggy Stardust was riveting because no one had ever seen a performer as confident in himself and his choices. In the D.A. Pennebaker documentary of the 3 July 1973 concert, Bowie not only nailed the concert, but did so with a supremely relaxed self-possession.[130] He never looked as if he were laboring either artistically or technically. It all came so easy to the lucky bastard. Bowie's mastery of the concert did not dissuade him from retiring the Ziggy Stardust character that night. Subsequent Bowie personas were an equal pitting of confidence and casualness. His "plastic soul" period won him an appearance on the black-oriented music show *Soul Train* after the album *Young Americans* (1975) vouched for Bowie's devotion to Philly soul. But Bowie dropped that mantle somewhere in the middle of *Station To Station* (1976), and with no sentimentality, took up with Krautrock in his next projects, the so-called Berlin trilogy of *Low*, *"Heroes"*, and *Lodger*. Although Bowie's roots were undeniably working-class, his breezy attitude toward stylistic renewal was more that of a wealthy person, the sort for whom anxiety is a foreign concept. And who could fault him for his nonchalance? With his Peter O'Toole-quality looks and his voice that blossomed, ugly-duckling-like, from nasal glam sneering to one of the strongest and most emotional tenors in pop history, Bowie's was an invincible composure that belongs to those lucky few who have to contend only with first-world problems.

This is not to suggest that there was anything cheap about Bowie's identity changes. He had impeccable taste, and the technical brilliance to pull off all of his singing, and most of his aesthetic transformations.[131] He also had the good sense to hide any traces of *work* in his work. Consider the last three music videos he made, for "Blackstar" (2015), "Lazarus" (2016), and "Where Are We Now" (2013). "Blackstar" alludes to "Space Oddity", Bowie's single from 1969, with its images of a Major Tom-like astronaut, presumably dead on a distant planet. A group of modestly-dressed women has retrieved Tom's jewel-encrusted skull, and worship by dancing around it. Bowie himself appears, first blindfolded and shaking as if in a seizure or religious trance, then waving around a little black book like a Mao of the (no) future. With its music, "Blackstar" adjoins jazz, the Middle East, and rhythm and blues, and Bowie's voice, though audibly more fragile, has aged admirably. In "Lazarus", Bowie gapes and twitches with the frenzy of one who knows that death is near. And in "Where Are We Now", Bowie could have erred by taking the nostalgia in the lyrics too literally, by assuming too earnest or desperate an expression for the camera. Director Tony Oursler's choice to project his face onto a blank doll's head deflects any easy music-video clichés, accessing instead the discourse of installation art. Those of pop music's Brahmin caste can get away with such things.

It may sound as if I am arguing for some false stylistic homogeneity, which I am not. Rather, Bowie excelled at demonstrating the fungibility of pop style, the fact that style can be picked up and dropped without changing the storyline. A few other performers have also possessed the quality: Miles Davis, Johnny Cash, Serge Gainsbourg, and yes, perhaps Madonna. All these artists could reinvent themselves stylistically because they all remained faithful to their fundamental identity, for which style was incidental, not essential. It is this quality that is now gone from pop, because the grand style, to deform Hegel, is not to have any particular style.[132] Bowie's stylistic transformations all shared Bowie's underlying indomitable confidence, a cool assertion that style itself was peripheral to Bowie. This does not mean that style was less important in Bowie's cosmology, but rather that style by definition was that which enclosed and clothed the essential.

So what, if anything, in the pop-music industry has been extinguished, and how is Bowie's departure related to that extinction? We have some obvious targets: phonographic media have come and gone and returned once again, from vinyl to compact cassette to compact disc to digital files. These technological upgrades have of course altered how recordings are created, distributed, and sold. The Napster peer-to-peer file-sharing debacle that culminated in the company's shutdown in 2001 did not result in the collapse of the music industry, although by the mid-2000s, this seemed a credible threat. But subscription services and platforms that allow free listening have rendered former patterns of listening and taste formation nearly unrecognizable. The fiction is that music is dying out, but fact is not especially far off. Pop music, at least as it existed for those born before 1980, has already become extinct. Bowie had a part to play in these changes, and it is sobering to reflect that a career of Bowie's longevity and proliferation would be impossible for any artist starting out today. So Bowie's legacy could be not only as a trailblazer but also as the last superstar of his kind, the one luckiest and most capable member of his artform (i.e. post-WWII popular music) to possess that talent, beauty, glamour, and nonchalance. If pop as we used to know it has gone the way of the dinosaur, it has been supplanted by an effervescence of creative anachronism, of pop artists who assume mythic or fictive or alternative identities. Bowie is clearly the point of reference here as well, although the stakes of stylistic transformation are lower now than during Bowie's career. Phylogeny has demonstrated that the dinosaurs did not die out, but rather evolved into birds. Bowie's metamorphoses linger to this day, but the perils of such changes are far reduced.

My ill-defined sense of loss at Bowie's passing is due not only to the fact that he was a public figure who represented late-capitalist decadence. Bowie was the scion of an entire aesthetic economy that privileged some materials at the expense of others, a pyramidal musical structure in which styles could be exchanged with one another to express boredom, joy, or any of the other sentiments that a nonchalant superpower enjoys the privilege of feeling. Bowie's changes laid out the metaphysical terrain of the artwork in crystalline concision, by emphasizing the interchangeable nature of style, and understating the centrality of substance. What we have lost in losing Bowie, what is different now thanks to new sound-alikes and the "Blurred Lines" verdict, is all this terrain. Style is now intellectual property and, at least in terms of the law, is as important as the aspects of a work like melody and lyrics that were previously essence. Style and content are now one, which means that content is everywhere, and appearance has been divested of the superficiality that Bowie so eloquently exploited. This is not to suggest that there are no artists today who attempt to play with style as Bowie did, nor that music today is worse than it was in the 1970s. The shifts derive rather from law and retromania. Law now provides a means for commodifying style by disallowing stylistic exchange. And retromania so pervades popular culture that it is difficult to locate pop music that doesn't sound like anything that came before. But retromania's roots extend beyond creative products to permeate the very conditions for making sense of pop. By default, any artist today, from Madonna to Lady Gaga to Flying Lotus to Beyoncé, who manipulates image and changes personas, is indexed under Bowie. Even if their stylistic shifts are distinct from Bowie's, the gesture of making them connects them to the past. No one can win in the quest for originality, because it has become our habit to make sense of music on the basis of its connections to the past. Less of this pressure, and surely less technological affordance, existed in the 1970s, and so while it was clear to many that Bowie had listened to 1950s rock 'n' roll and urban blues like many other postwar Brits, it was far from clear how he could pass from glam to plastic soul to electronica to black dance music in only ten years. So, what I mourn in mourning Bowie is not only the man and his music, but the experience of hearing, for the first and last time, stylistic jumps and appropriations that were simply too new to contextualize.

As way of a coda, there is one other artist, thankfully still alive in 2016, whose stylistic changes have been similar to Bowie's at least in terms of their latent assertion of style as accident. Consider the career of Scott Walker, an American baritone singer and pop instrumentalist who moved to London in the mid-1960s to pursue his career and avoid the Vietnam draft. Walker's earliest hits were with his group, The Walker Brothers, and they were a motley assemblage of middle-of-the-road Motown derivatives and Broadway torch songs. By Walker's own admission[133], there was plenty of style (thanks to Walker's miraculous voice) but little substance, if by substance we mean resistant aesthetic or political content. Walker's first period was a series of beautifully-crafted hits intended for chart success, with lush accompaniments and lyrics inevitably about romance. The interchangeability of these songs' styles – country or schmaltzy pop or soul – was slightly unnerving. Walker at this point didn't perform many of his own compositions, and the most revolutionary music he did perform consisted of arrangements of the work of Jacques Brel, their trenchant lyrics translated into mid-1960s argot.

This changes with Walker's four solo albums, which feature more of his original music and verses with each successive iteration. The lion's share of critical adulation gathers around *Scott 4* (1969), but the flame was first lit as early as the first album, *Scott* (1967). Listen to "Such A Small Love", which is more of a piece with mid-twentieth-century film soundtracks or experimental music than with pop ballads. Its distant high strings seethe tremulously as Walker's voice enters, his lyrics reflecting on a brief, failed romance. Its impressionistic, stream-of-consciousness poetry tilts toward obscurity, until the full strings flood in, and Walker croons the title phrase with his perfect voice. Here was an early sighting of the Scott Walker who would become the hero for the next four decades of indie-pop elite, from Julian Cope and Bowie to Jarvis Cocker and Radiohead. The industry's grip on Walker's talent began to be pried off, finger by finger. By *Scott 4*, some fans wrote off Walker, convinced that their idol had lost the plot. But the other sort of fan, the one who will calmly state that Walker is the single most important musician of his generation, regard *Scott 4* as his first mature artistic output. A struggle with depression and alcoholism, and the banal, financial pressures of family life, compelled Walker to perform in dive venues in the early 1970s, and to release some throwaway country and easy-listening albums. This was the bottoming out of Walker's career, a moment of molting where the schmaltz briefly coexisted with the album *Nite Flights* (1978), one-part visionary songs to two-parts the same pop drivel. After *Nite Flights*, Walker waited six years before releasing his next album *Climate of Hunter* (1984). This album marked Walker's permanent disengagement with the hit industry, and his full-time engagement with the avant-garde via the conventions of pop and classical music. What is so assaulting about *Climate of Hunter* is that Walker assumes different masks of pop music, always with explicit recognition of their artificiality. The opening ballad, "Rawhide", for instance, begins with the sounds of a lone cowbell struck seemingly at random internals; the sound pans slowly from right to left channels. Then the electric bass, keyboards, and drums enter, and Walker sings, "This is how you disappear". The drums and bass anchor the track in early-1980s production, Walker's verses are enigmatic, and synthesized strings point toward classical or soundtrack composition. "Rawhide" points in three different directions at once, then, and fades out before any of the three are allowed to develop.

What unites Walker's mature output, from *Scott* through the present, are a handful of concrete technical elements. For instance, "Boy Child" (1969), "Dealer" and "Sleepwalker's Woman" (1984), and "Bouncer See Bouncer..." (1995) visit if not reside in the Lydian mode, Walker's preferred area for evoking dreams and contingency. "The Electrician" (1978) and "Herod 2014" (2014) go to the darkest acts of humanity, from torture to infanticide. And despite all of these unsettling quirks, the other constant is Walker's voice, older and somewhat weaker, (he was seventy-one years old at the release of his most recent album, *Soused*), but with its vibrato and pathos and unearthly allure fully intact. If Bowie's true self was confidence and episodic conviction, Walker's is an ungainly combination of technical perfection and disaffection with that perfection. Walker's self-critiques are widely known; he has all but disowned his commercial music of the early 1970s as artistic sin, a lazy reliance on his voice and pop fashion. His true voice repudiates anything that is easy, whether that is blind adherence to convention or blind reliance on his voice, or renunciation of that voice. Listen to "Brando", the opening track from *Soused*, his collaboration with drone metal group Sunn 0))). There is the abrupt, breathtaking beginning in which an organ and Walker, higher in his baritone than fans are used to hearing him, proffer an image. "Ah, the wide Missouri!", Walker cries, and we are swept along with the majestic scene even as a grungy electric guitar responds with its own sort of affirmation. After a few more statements like this, the track then descends into the paranoia typical both of Sunn 0))) drones as well as Walker's later work. Vocals are infrequent, lyrics are oblique, referring to Brando's apparent penchant for roles in which he is physically beaten. A reprise of the opening occurs later in the song, but it comes too late, and far too much darkness has been exposed in the meantime, for the panoramic music to offer any solace. This track could be described as drone music, as experimental rock, as musical theater, as horrorcore, or as some other style. Or, we could simply call it electronic music, for the reason that its sounds are unthinkable without electronic instruments and processing tools. Obviously, there are the instruments of drone here, Sunn 0)))'s electric guitars and synthesizers, rendering sustained, loud, noisy sounds that would be unattainable through acoustic means. But there is also Walker's voice, recorded with a close microphone in a relatively voluminous acoustic to sound utterly alone and bare. Electronics make it possible for us to hear the control and sensitivity and flaws of Walker's voice. And so, Walker's voice in "Brando" could be heard as a product of electronic music, or even as an electronic instrument, for he would certainly not sound as strong or as naked without the intervention of the studio. Walker's decisions since *Nite Flights* have amounted to making amends for the great beauty of his voice, which he buries beneath such unconventional sounds as meat-punching[134] or whip-cracking.[135]

A truth of the careers of Bowie and Walker, or Miles Davis or Tom Waits or any other musician of the later twentieth century, is that historical singularity makes their music so compelling. This may sound too Hegelian, like some declaration of the end of music. But market forces, technologies, methods of consuming art – all these factors culminated in a series of genuinely novel, original artists. These factors tilt today in favor of copying rather than originality, and style happens to be the preferred currency of that transaction. Thus, a technically brilliant contemporary band like Shearwater moves me with its song "Snow Leopard" (2008), but I can't help being reminded that lead singer Jonathan Meiburg's voice is similar to Bryan Ferry's, or that the song sounds like Roxy Music. (It doesn't hurt that Shearwater is currently touring, as their encore set, all of Bowie's album *Lodger*, from 1979.) And the inert depression of Songs: Ohia can't help but recall for me the suicidal poise of Nick Drake. My generation, at this point in the twenty-first century, is in for a series of blows as those who first taught us to love and dream and live through art pass away. Those artists today who model themselves on the style of the past are condemned to be compared to that past. There can be no second Bowie, even though thousands might cite him as an inspiration.

A Society for Creative Anachronism

Reynolds' *Retromania* ends on a subdued note. While there are certainly hopeful aspects to retro pop – Reynolds singles out Boards of Canada and Daniel Lopatin for commendation – the phenomenon bespeaks complacency. Reynolds is too observant to fall victim to the propaganda of originality and progress, and he rightly points out several past iterations of futurism that enlisted more talk than action. Still, aside from dubstep, the electronica genre he regards as veritably novel, Reynolds concludes in stating that pop is eating its tail in an infatuation with past glories.[136]

This is a valid criticism, especially considering that styles are being recreated wholesale in sound-alikes. But amid all this retromania, we can find sizeable pockets of "creative anachronism", or artistic re-imaginings of the past.[137] Reynolds may well be right in diagnosing this ocean of pastness as aesthetic and even spiritual regression, or at least the opposite of progress, of courage. But for participants and enthusiasts, creative anachronism is dialectically related to, or even symptomatic of, the belief that music is becoming extinct. This essay is intended not as a refutation of Reynolds' book, whose conclusions are unimpeachable. This might well be urging that we see the glass as half-full. Reynolds is far from the only one to believe in the thought-fiction that pop music is dying out, or at least foundering, sinking in the ocean of seemingly infinite choice and instantaneous recall. *Future historians of the early twenty-first century will think, I'd like to believe, that we did the best we could with the sudden onset of technologies, like digital audio files and cellphones, for which we were ill-prepared. Some of us acted like adolescents, using the internet for easy thrills. But others lost the plot in the best possible way, by imagining alternative endings, unlikely offspring, and fictive languages.*[138] This essay attempts to give those visionaries their due.

* *

Mark Kate is an electronica artist based in San Francisco. He released the album *Despairer* in March 2016. Kate sells his music both online through Bandcamp as well as in physical editions like compact disc, vinyl, and cassette. At his album release event, Kate was surprised that he sold more cassette copies of his work than any other format, physical or digital.[139] This is not an isolated case, at least in niche genres like electronica or punk or any genre not conceived primarily for hit success. Tape was a lucrative phonographic medium from the late 1970s through the early 1990s. But cassettes were acknowledged as acoustically inferior to vinyl, and were less durable than either vinyl or compact disc. The timing of the arrival of compact discs starting in 1982 meant that cassettes enjoyed only ten or so years of widespread usage, after which they rapidly became a second choice for consumers.

So far, I am setting up a trajectory familiar enough to be the butt of an extended joke about hipsters (in *Portlandia*'s music-video sequence for "The Dream of the 1890s").[140] Millennials and youngish generation-X'ers take up an antiquated practice, from beards to truckers hats to artisanal foods – sausages, pickles, breads, milk or eggs from domestically farmed livestock. In so doing, they reject corporate culture and relive the simple pleasures of their grandparents' generation. Cassette tapes are by no means a product of the 1890s, but given the ubiquity of digital music and its promises of "lossless", eternal fidelity, cassettes might as well have come from the nineteenth century. Although one of their allures during the 1980s was their relative portability (compared to vinyl, at any rate), they can seem hopelessly bulky by today's standards, as well as fickle, delicate, and sonically mediocre. Hipsters' willingness to rediscover tape might be too easily summed up as affectation.

To their defense, hipsters have some reason for nostalgia for tape. The medium existed both as prerecorded tapes of music or other acoustic content and as blank tapes. Some tape recorders were sold as "boomboxes" bundled with radios, allowing tape recording straight from the radio. Dual-cassette players allowed dubbing of tapes, which facilitated piracy. One of the most eloquent meditations on the possibilities of the two-cassette recorder is the passage in Nick Hornby's novel, *High Fidelity*, that discusses the rules of the mixtape. The protagonist Rob explains the mixtape as a covert love letter, a means of expressing attraction while safely hiding behind rock songs. Rob lists some of the rules of mixtape assemblage, from tempo to genre to the racial make-up of its musicians.[141] Although a tape dub is undeniably of lesser acoustic quality than an original recording, it could be good enough to introduce to a friend or love interest a beloved song. Blank cassette tapes ushered in a sort of epistolary musical culture.

But there were undeniable problems with tapes, as well. A tape is only as good as its tape player, and playback depends on steadiness of power source. Listening to a tape player that was plugged into alternating current (AC) was more reliable than listening to a battery-powered machine, for which playback speed would vary according to how much battery power remained. Tapes were sensitive to extremes in temperature, and so could not be left in a hot car. Machines in less than perfect repair could simply stop reading a particular register or timbral area, leading to the unsettling experience of listening to a song for which the voice or a single instrument is only faintly audible or even absent altogether, while the rest of the music continues at a normal volume. In retrospect, the irregularities and temperamental nature of tape playback furnished an unpredictable, even exciting listening experience. But high fidelity, it was not.

The cassette tape also had its quirks. It was the first medium that more or less encouraged hacking. On many commercially released tapes, the left and right ends of the top side of the box contained two square indentations. Left unchanged, these niches prevented the tape player from recording over the sounds on the tape. Covering these dents with Scotch tape enabled the tape recorder to record over the material, converting a unidirectional medium into one that made possible audio collage as well as complete effacement of the material underneath. Depending on the quality of tape cassette and tape player, sound material on one side could "bleed over" onto the other. This was too rare to be a glitch worth fixing, and would be audible only with the right conjunction of silence on the side being played, with loud material on the reverse side. The result was unearthly, a mere shadow of music played in reverse (since forward play on Side A means a retreat on Side B, and vice versa), smoky and ill-defined, but nonetheless recognizable to someone who spent enough time with the tape. And let's not forget the built-in inconvenience of a tape's topography. Unlike vinyl or compact discs, tapes cannot be played at any point instantaneously. They can be rewound or advanced through the fast-forward function, and these processes themselves exert wear-and-tear on the magnetic dust that encodes the sound, as well as the tape itself. Let's also consider this magnetic dust, the substrate by which sound can be transmitted on tape. Much has been said about William Basinski's magnum opus from 2001, *The Disintegration Loops*, which uses the degradation of tape dust as a point of departure for his gradually disappearing works.[142] But before Basinski repurposed this technical weakness into an aesthetic process, it was simply an annoyance for anyone during the 1980s who bought a tape only to hear that successive listening was slowly effacing the sound.[143]

All of these charms and peccadilloes of cassette tapes do little, in my mind, to explain why niche-genre enthusiasts and hipsters would want to rediscover or reinvest in the medium. The revival of vinyl records, also a phenomenon prevalent among listeners to various sorts of electronica, is understandable because vinyl records provide a warm analog sound that is often absent on digital compact discs, and especially in mp3s and other compressed audio formats. A return to vinyl, for either old or new music, is a return to a putatively better acoustic experience. But a return to cassette is a bit like a return to a stick-shift transmission, or black-and-white television without cable. Its rewards may have less to do with nostalgia, since many of the consumers of tape today may not have even been born by the time cassettes disappeared from the marketplace. Instead, the revival posits the fiction that we lost something important in letting go of tape, a *memento mori* that today's formats, with their blandishments of permanence, refuse to accept.

The strange result of this revival is that cassettes are experiencing an appreciation they never received their first time around. Independent artists with relatively small audiences are releasing cassettes. So are mainstream powerhouses like Justin Bieber (the album *Purpose*, from 2015) and Kanye West (the album *Yeezus*, from 2013). That major stars should choose to jump on the hipster bandwagon is another confirmation that the pop industry is encouraging listeners to curate their experiences. In choosing an antiquated format, especially one with so many idiosyncrasies, a listener furnishes her internal listening salon with memories fake or genuine, subcultural capital, and a format of restricted circulation that encloses what would otherwise be an overwhelming ocean of choice.

For that is the crux of the matter, that we are intoxicated by choice and niche-genres and formats and customizable experiences. If the fiction introduced at the beginning of this essay is that tape is dying, the reality is that tape never had it so good. Retromania is a concept absolutely beholden on fictions of finitude and morbidity and scarcity. The allure of tape, or genres like hauntology or activities like concert recreations, is that they are resuscitating what had already expired. But death is the opposite of the wild flourishing of the antiquated that we are witnessing.

* *

The first contact with Actually Huizenga's work should be with her music videos. As talented a songwriter and singer as she is, her strong suit is her odd video art, equal parts softcore porn, slasher and other horror-niche cinema, DIY website design from the 1990s, and experimental film in the tradition of Kenneth Anger. Bracketing out the visual in order to access some musical essence to Huizenga's work would be missing the point.

We can take the video for "Predator Romantic" as a starting point. In no particular sequential or logical order, Huizenga lays out several topics, many of which are examples of retromania. The first setting is the beach, where waves wash over a miniature piano figurine. An androgynous man with long dark hair and reptilian contact lenses lip-syncs to the camera a line spoken by Arnold Schwarzenegger from the 1987 film *Predator*: "If it bleeds, we can kill it." The music enters, a mid-tempo dance track whose shuffle ostinato recalls the tango. There are intermittent synthesizer flourishes, a standard drum set with kick and snare, and treated electric guitar. Huizenga's overdubbed voice enters, describing a man who enjoys blood and kink in his love-making. The visual rhythm of the video falls into a groove as new images rise and fall about every two to three seconds. Some of these images are superimposed, strafed, and magnified on top of others. Other images fill the frame and are stationary; these are a sort of background or canvas. And oh, what images! Huizenga is clothed alternately as a shepherdess, a dominatrix in vampire or Viking style, and a sexpot à la Madonna in her *Like A Virgin* period. (Madonna looms as a reference here.) The set piece on the beach, with Huizenga dripping from the surf and flanked by a male dancer, recalls the choreography of "Lucky Star" and the locale of "Cherish". And Huizenga's voice, migrating between an earthy alto and a girlish falsetto, recalls both "Live To Tell" and "Material Girl".

All of these visual and audio elements are superimposed, embodying what Carol Vernallis terms the "swirl" of recent digital new media.[144] Huizenga piles it on; just take the references to 1980s culture and the sheer visual surfeit, and the result is already vertiginous. But there is also the shock value, and the true feat here is that Huizenga maintains a consistent salaciousness not only in "Predator Romantic", but in all of her videos. For Huizenga is a burlesque performer as much as a musician and filmmaker. She is A-list beautiful, with blond curly hair, blue eyes, and doll-like features. She is also centerfold beautiful (her mother was a Playboy bunny), with a curvaceous body that she shows in various states of near-nudity and kink: holding a goat or snake or guinea pig as if they were objects of affection; stroking the cheek of a bound man with a knife-claw, deeply enough to draw (possibly real) blood; herself with arms bound and a metal instrument that forces her jaw open; ballet point shoes and princess dresses, enjoying a banquet with surfers and genies. Huizenga appears in a few shots covered with a white powder that could be powdered sugar or cocaine, and a male counterpart licks her belly clean. Later, she appears in a barn, holding a goat and kept company by two muscular men dressed in loin cloths and satyr costumes. There are passing shots of Roman-style mosaics as well. A distillation of these topical areas yields the following categories: the bacchanalia; the horror film; bondage and discipline subculture; the film *Predator*; silent-film-era cliché (the bound victim, the genie with Rudolf Valentino-like looks). And while the music follows a standard verse/chorus alternation and thus adheres to a predictable timing of events, the editing of these visual topics is muddled and quick. The frequent superimposition of graphics (in outmoded cut-and-paste style) means that distinctions between topics are aggressively worn down. This is swirl in the truest sense.

"Predator Romantic" simmers at a fever pitch of smut. But it is hardly gratuitous. Remember the defense of Madonna in the

1980s and 1990s, that her sexualized roles were subversive rather than demeaning because they wrested control of the male gaze?[145] The argument could be rewritten with Huizenga's work in mind, in such a way that Madonna seems positively patriarchal in comparison. For Madonna and her progeny, Nicki Minaj, Miley Cyrus, and Lily Allen, merely mimic libido and desire, in order to critique them. This is a version of the "if you can't beat 'em" (i.e. the objectifying male viewer), "then join 'em" (i.e. by inviting him to look, but on your terms). Huizenga on the other hand presents a much more unsettling prospect. For she is an artist who really does exert total creative control over sound and image (and costuming and casting and editing and other less glamourous aspects of video art.) She places herself in debasing evocations of bestiality, fetishism, sacrilege, gluttony, and does so while clearly communicating enjoyment and humor, even joy. (I suspect that at least one love scene in her corpus is not acted, but the real thing.) Huizenga's delight, the lack of irony in her delivery, puts her more in line with 1950s bondage starlet Betty Page than Madonna. And here is the truly subversive element in Huizenga's fantasy: not that she shows such perverse situations, but that her enjoyment of such situations is so unperverse, so untroubled.

Judging only from "Predator Romantic", at least from its excellent song, we might say that Huizenga is a pop star who is treating the banal topics of desire and objectification, albeit with images that are at once more shocking and more amusing. But "Predator Romantic" is the most conventional of Huizenga's videos, not in terms of its content, but rather its format. Compare it to "Viking Angel", a video lasting over thirty minutes that contains four music videos embedded in it, plus connective scenes and transitional material. This hybridity makes it difficult to ascribe to it any one genre designation. There are narrative film elements that thin about halfway through: Huizenga plays a young aspiring actress coerced onto the casting couch by a roué producer. Meanwhile, the police are searching for a serial killer who preys on starlets, and the detective assigned to the case grows obsessed with Huizenga. The film concludes in a narrative and literal mess. Huizenga finds herself in a dodgy Hollywood mansion whose attendees look like porn stars or filmmakers. What starts out as an orgy degenerates into a satanic ritual with Huizenga as the intended sacrificial victim, only she grabs a knife and slits the throat of her assailant. In passing, there are seemingly unrelated appearances by construction workers, a Tarzan-like muscle man, even a man twirling a road-sign that reads "Sacrifice here". There are both snarky and sinister references to L.A. and Hollywood throughout, from a close-up of the infamous newspaper photo of the Black Dahlia murder victim, to a close-up of Bruce Willis, and from a parody of the louche casting couch creep to a send-up of vapid local newscasters describing gory details. Nothing in the material flags "Viking Angel" as "serious" art, art that takes itself too seriously. And yet the salacious content sequesters "Viking Angel" and her other work from mainstream media coverage. Standards are certainly laxer than they were in previous decades, but Huizenga's blood orgies won't make it onto MTV any time soon.

We thus have a pop artist thoroughly steeped in retromania by Reynolds' standards, yet whose content recuses her from substantial commercial success. Huizenga's work possesses "discursive accents", a concept I've elsewhere proposed for audiovisual indices to genres.[146] Here, we encounter accents of various vernacular film niches, but also pop and avant-garde video. The latter element is even more pronounced in "Softrock" (2011), Huizenga's collaboration with photographer Socrates Mitsios. "Softrock" is distant from any familiar model of pop-music video because its soundtrack is almost exclusively sound rather than music, and what music there is consists of drones and disturbingly liminal noise. Bereft of any clear narrative, it shows mostly slow-motion images of Huizenga's face as she looks up suggestively at Mitsios. In other shots, Mitsios has sex with Huizenga from behind, sometimes pushing her head down or even off the bed. It is heavily-charged material that marshals anxieties of domestic abuse and rape, voyeurism and surveillance. The mediated frames and image quality invoke Super 8 video cameras, and with the vaguely disquieting sound, I am reminded of David Lynch's *Lost Highway* (1997). But unlike Lynch films which regale in the suffering of sexualized females, "Softrock" plays the same card as "Predator Romantic". Huizenga does not ever seem to suffer in her sex scenes, in "Softrock" or elsewhere; to the contrary, she seems genuinely to enjoy them.

The question of audience is always a challenging one in popular-music criticism, and never more so than today, where style has been rendered into just one more switch on the producer's metaphorical mixing console. If it ever were possible to extrapolate an intended audience for any pop track, we could do so only imperfectly, because audiences seek and create meaning in music that was not produced with them in mind. Still, commerce is commerce, and the fact that Huizenga's opus contains discursive accents inclining toward light pop and pulp/B-movie cinema suggests that a pop audience, however defined, is at least one target constituency for the work. Other accents recall the gore art of Paul McCarthy or Hermann Nitsch, or the feminist critique of Cindy Sherman, and so the work may also lean toward experimental and avant-garde camps. We could conclude that Huizenga wants both the prestige of the avant-garde and the pleasure of retro-pop. However informed such a conclusion might be, I feel that it misses the point. There is a surging, seething creativity in Huizenga's sacrilegious potions, which are so incommensurate with pop success. I can only conclude that she does what she does because she loves it, because it creates new worlds of thought, and not because it is critique, or nostalgia, or pathos. If music like Huizenga's tells of extinction, it is one that is coupled with a resurgence and willingness to try something new.

* *

The model of retromania is one ultimately premised on the full awareness of the ramifications of turning to the past. Reynolds regards it as a dismal fate for culture because he, and a great many other musicians and artists, have personal associations with each evocation of the past. Each quotation and reference is laden with affective weight, which well explains the heaviness and lugubriousness of some hauntology music. But scholars, in their haste to respect audiences and musicians alike, might be skipping a crucial question: do the artists and audiences of a creatively anachronistic work care about its invocations of the past?

Let's think about another recent celebrity death, that of Christopher Lee, who passed in 2015. Amid the tributes to his work as an actor (most famously, as Count Dracula in numerous Hammer films, and as villains in the *Lord of the Rings* and *Star Wars* franchises), I was fortunate enough to hear a local college radio station play one of his collaborations with heavy-metal musicians. This track was called "The Magic of the Wizard's Dream", written and performed by the Italian symphonic metal group Rhapsody of Fire. It begins in a style reminiscent of the opening to Led Zeppelin's "Stairway to Heaven", with acoustic guitar and Baroque flute tracing a modally-tinged minor-key melody germane to Renaissance fairs. Rhapsody of Fire's vocalist Alex Staropoli sings of darkness and wanting to find one's way before Lee's tremulous bass enters, singing of fate and honor with a gravitas worthy of Verdi. The ensuing song is a poem to mythological or fantastical creatures who could have stepped out of a Tolkein novel. To my jaded sensibilities, it seemed like a send-up, a hilarious combination of metal with kitschy operatic pretention.

But interviews with Lee and members of Rhapsody of Fire as well as viewer comments on YouTube indicate that irony is largely absent, at least among those who sincerely like the track.[147]

It's difficult to know what to make of "The Magic of the Wizard's Dream". I laughed at it when I first saw it but also loved it, because I felt that it attained that elusive variant of kitsch, the state of being so-bad-that-it's-good. But my appreciation of the irony may not be appropriate here. I assumed that Lee and Rhapsody of Fire were putting forth a parody of heavy metal worthy of *This Is Spinal Tap*. But in an interview, Lee is clearly not poking fun of symphonic metal; to the contrary, he gives a clear impression of enjoying and being proud of his evocation of Charlemagne's rule.[148] A traditional tactic for making sense of such postmodern appropriations, following Fredric Jameson, is to assume that artists borrow from the past ahistorically, simply for the thrill of the arcane.[149] Neither ironic distance nor ignorance accounts for the retromania at play here, though. Lee, in the video for his own song "The Bloody Verdict of Verden", is dressed as Charlemagne amid low-budget green-screen sets of crumbling castles and piles of bones. He points his longsword toward the camera as he recounts Charlemagne's execution of over four-thousand Saxon pagans, a historical event that took place in 782. It is kitschy anachronistic fun, but it is not cynical. Houellebecq dubs this tendency "heroic fantasy"[150], and it belies the stagnation that Reynolds perceives in retromania. It is a generative act, and whatever our personal judgment of its aesthetic merit, we have to admit that it is not undertaken with any sense of death or defeat in mind.

So what is this "heroic fantasy", and why is it a viable alternative to retromania? It could easily be discounted as kitsch, but kitsch implies naiveté. At play here is a knowing, purposeful affection for mythological and grandiose images. It is not a liability that such images draw from past traditions, because the creativity lies in how these images are then reassembled. Even this account does not go far enough, for there is the sentiment of sincerity, of honest belief in the quality and purpose of the work that is paramount. Let's think about Sigur Rós, the Icelandic rock group, whose early recordings contained lyrics in an invented language called "Hopelandish".[151] This ease with fiction is well-paired with Sigur Rós tracks like those on the ( ) album of 2002, which apply indie rock idioms (e.g. extended song forms, avoidance of the standard verse/chorus/bridge structure, rock drums but no guitar solos, ambient soundscapes, etc.) to epic, soaring melodies and brooding, somber harmonies. Sigur Rós' music has been described as a musical embodiment of Iceland, a fitting counterpart to its Viking history and geological peculiarities and breath-catching beauty. The critical goodwill shown towards such traits, fixtures that the original punks might have derived as romantic, speaks volumes. We have progressed in pop beyond the uptight rejection of kitsch and pleasure. Sigur Rós and their fans are not afraid to admit that they enjoy a beautiful melody, or legends and tales of heroism. (Sigur Rós briefly appeared as a trio of musicians in an episode of *Game of Thrones*.[152])

Invented languages used to be considered signs of despair. Hugo Ball's absurdly tubular costume for his Cabaret Voltaire show was of a piece with his nonsense poem "Karawane"[153], and with Kurt Schwitters' *Ursonate*, a spoken-word poem in which nonsense syllables are organized to form the first movement of a sonata, complete with first and second themes in the exposition, a development, and a recapitulation.[154] The Dadaist abnegation of beauty, truth, and reason permeates this language, which is deconstructed, split into elementary particles, and anatomized. The destruction of 1914–18 so hardened the hearts of the Dadaists and their descendants – the Situationists, the soixante-huitards, and the punks – that even faith in the basic communicative capacity of language was lost. But invented languages featured in the pop of heroic fantasy spring from a different source. Sigur

Rós was prefigured by the Cocteau Twins, whose singer Elizabeth Frazer often sang in a Gaelic-inflected invented language. Before the Cocteau Twins, there was the 1970s French progressive rock band Magma, which used its own invented language in songs about a fictive world called Kobaïa. Whatever the details of Magma's unearthly world, their musical gestures are familiar: rock drumming punctuated by extended solos by percussionist and vocalist Christian Vander; progressive rock guitar and keyboard solos; compound meters and jazz modulations; long extended instrumental jams. Magma throws us headfirst into the conventions of mind-expanding freak-out music, and everything here departs from an implicit faith in progress, growth, and enlightenment. And the singing! Vander is as meticulous in his articulation as any capable performer of the *Ursonate,* dancing over vertiginously rapid syllables with seemingly no effort. But unlike any Dadaist virtuoso, Vander enjoys the challenge, and delivers the lines as if they were Rossini or Verdi or even sacred scripture. The act of creating a fictitious language and a cosmology to support it entails so many other creative decisions. Explaining a social system requires a mythology, a means of telling why things are just so. A new language requires not only distinct words, but grammar and syntax, and above all the certainty that such a language can signify. This alone is the most creative and heroic of anachronisms.

I have cast a cheerful light on the preceding examples of creative anachronism, stressing the optimism it requires to invent a new identity or language. Creative anachronism treats history as an *à la carte* menu from which the artist selects elements to carve out a new life. These specific examples telegraph hope rather than nostalgia or melancholy. They nonetheless affirm Reynolds' diagnosis of retromania, because they accept as their starting point the need to quit the present in order to arrive at some exotic future. What distinguishes creative anachronism from brooding hauntology or the other examples cited by Reynolds is a pleasure at wandering in a fictive mental geography. I want to conclude this essay by turning to a group that engaged in a sort of creative anachronism with an outlook far less sanguine. Some of the same tropes of retromania apply here: free borrowing from multiple historical moments, and a construction of a new mythology, a backstory, if you will. But unlike the previous examples, the artists here do not create their anachronism with visible joy. Their inability to explain their motives suggests that this fiction was undertaken in despair at the future of music.

The story of The KLF has been thoroughly documented by the band itself and their publicists as well as in John Higgs' book, so I touch on their most salient acts here only in passing.[155] The KLF (also known as The JAMs, or Justified Ancients of Mu Mu) was a British pop duo consisting of Bill Drummond and Jimmy Cauty. Starting in the late 1980s, their professed goal was to make hit records, and they excelled at this despite or even because of their unapologetic honesty. The KLF's first tracks sampled well-known pop songs such as ABBA's "Dancing Queen", a move that resulted in a copyright complaint. (Drummond and Cauty eventually burned all remaining copies of the offending album in order to placate ABBA and their lawyers.) Litigation notwith-standing, The KLF scored several hits, including their *Dr. Who* homage, "Doctorin' The Tardis", in 1988 (released under an alternative stage name, The Timelords). Drummond and Cauty soon after published *The Manual: How to Have a Number One Hit the Easy Way*, a step-by-step guide on how to produce and market a hit record.[156] This sounds cynical and perhaps it was, but several readers went on to credit *The Manual* for their own success. In 1992 The KLF released its single, "Stand By The JAMs", which featured country superstar Tammy Wynette. Stylistically, the song was essentially a combination of acid house and hiphop, with sampled female backup voices and an up-tempo basic four-beat march. The music video, however, points in any number of directions. There are Asian women in blonde wigs dressed as angels who beckon toward a boat, Drummond and Cauty themselves wearing hooded capes and horns, a strange island with vaguely Atlantean imagery, and Wynette in a Nashville-royalty dress singing of the justified ancients who will one day return in righteousness. Drummond and Cauty explained the song as a treatment of the mythic lost civilization of Mu which supposedly disappeared under the Atlantic Ocean in the distant past. (The civilization of Mu is itself a thought-fiction.) The KLF also appeared at the 1992 Brit Awards, performing with death-metal group Extreme Noise Terror. Drummond took the stage in a kilt, black leather jacket, and crutches, and after singing a few verses, shot blanks from a vintage machine gun at the audience. That same night, The KLF also had thrown at the steps of the Brit Award venue a dead sheep, pinned with a message that read, "I died for you [sic, ewe]".

The KLF's most notorious act was their 1994 burning of a million pounds in cash, the proceeds from their record sales. Drummond and Cauty videorecorded themselves throwing stacks of fifty-pound bills into the fire. The act was discounted as a hoax, and when it was shown conclusively (through forensic testing!) that the money was indeed destroyed, critics responded even more harshly, complaining that the act was irresponsible given that the money could have been used to help those in need. Higgs' book and much of the journalism devoted to The KLF has focused on the destruction of the money, but I want to reconsider an earlier event that took place on the Summer Solstice of 1991, when Drummond and Cauty invited several international journalists to the Scottish island of Jura for a staged pseudo-pagan rite.[157] Drummond greeted the visitors disguised as a customs agent for the Mu civilization and speaking an invented language, stamping their passports with the so-called K Foundation's symbol, loudspeakers in front of a pyramid. The K

Foundation was what Drummond and Cauty called themselves when they expanded their activities beyond making hit records to the production of art. As such, The K Foundation aimed for the channels of high art, but engaged in radical critiques of capitalism. They also created a mythology comprised of elements from the recently invented religion known as Discordianism. The events at the solstice were documented in a film entitled "The Rites of Mu", featuring a voiceover narrator imitating Martin Sheen's performance in *Apocalypse Now*. All participants were outfitted with hooded white robes and were led to a sixty-foot wicker man, which was then set ablaze.

It's unclear how seriously journalists took the event as it was happening, but it's easy in retrospect to frame the Solstice rite as a hoax or stunt. Before doing so, we should consider Drummond's and Cauty's own thoughts on the happening. The two invented an entire belief system that drew on pagan ritual, concocted legend, and the paranoid science fiction of Robert Anton Wilson's *Illuminatus!* trilogy of novels. Even this is not as surprising as the fact that Drummond and Cauty openly admit to having done all of this. They had no intention of duping anyone, and while the 1991 Solstice might be written off as a rather obvious grab at publicity and record sales, the pair was only too willing to dispense with any proceeds from the event when they burned their money in 1994. The purpose of The K Foundation's mythology was not to start a cult or sponsor a belief system. And if The K Foundation at times seemed dedicated to generating publicity, Drummond and Cauty did not seem overly concerned when, for instance, their burning of the money resulted in scant media attention. With complete transparency and with no clear motive, The K Foundation shone light on a thought-fiction, a fantasy of adulterated history and legend. According to the epilogue in "The Rites of Mu", the fourth handmaiden of the devil is the question "why?". The events of the solstice and, more broadly, the fabricated myths of The KLF beg this same question, but we could in turn ask "why?" of virtually any facet of pop music. Why do audiences ignore the artificial or alienating elements when they attend a concert, and how do they derive pleasure from them? Is there any difference between The K Foundation speaking of the lost continent of Mu and classic pop songs (like "Love Me Tender" or "My Generation") that speak of true love or teenage rebellion? Why is The K Foundation derided as a fraud while Elvis Presley and The Who are received as serious poets?

Let's also keep in mind the chronology in Drummond's and Cauty's activities. They began by referring to themselves as either The Justified Ancients of Mu Mu or The KLF in 1987; in 1988, they published *The Manual*. In 1990 they released the critically acclaimed *Chill Out* album, which spawned an entire subgenre of EDM. They burned the wicker man in 1991, and around that same time began to refer to themselves as The K Foundation, at first along with and later instead of The KLF. They burned the money in 1994. There aren't any clean borders to separate The KLF from The JAMs or The K Foundation, but there is a general progression from pop success to renunciation of that success. Drummond and Cauty have been candid about their disdain for the pop industry's avarice. Placing the fictions the industry promulgates – that talent emerges and is captured on a recording, that consumer choice alone determines which songs become hits, that pop is an original form of personal expression – in the center of The K Foundation's activities, and candidly admitting to profiting from those very fictions, Drummond and Cauty stick a needle in every pretension that keeps the industry afloat. The truth in The KLF's belief system is that pop music lost its integrity a long time ago. (There is an even greater truth to which Marx first alerted us, that capitalism functions thanks to the myth of money as a token of power.) And by that reasoning, if the enterprise is dead but people refuse to acknowledge it, art at least can recognize the emperor's nakedness.

So I close this essay feeling even more pessimistic than Reynolds, even though I began it with the intention of showing that creative anachronism had some redemptive qualities. Retromania is not reducible to creative anachronism, but the two take up a sizeable proportion of retromaniacal activities. And as any good politician knows, the best way to neutralize bad publicity is to spin it into good publicity. These various attempts at creative anachronism cut across stylistic divisions. Here alone, I've traced instances in dance pop (Huizenga), post-rock (Sigur Rós), progressive rock (Magma), and acid house (The KLF). Currently pop is fairly overflowing with other examples, from Miley Cyrus' deformation of her child-star pedigree, to Nick Minaj as a parody of male fantasies about women. Inevitably, these personas draw on older musical characteristics as well as vintage visual cues. But is the fact that such creative reimagining exists the only common element among such disparate practices? No, because there is in fact a common style to these appropriations of the past. It consists of invincibly upbeat, even joyous or comedic energy. Tempi here are frequently fast enough to suggest dancing. There is also a sense of humor in these identities, a sort of comic freedom that comes from being able to put on a mask and later take it off. The casual confidence, the joy, and the sense of play: these are all elements that draw from Bowie, and Bowie would probably add that he in turn got it from his childhood idols, Little Richard and Screaming Jay Hawkins. But the early rock 'n' rollers made up new identities, like the transsexual screamer and the revenant rocker, that had no point of reference in music. These were crazy ravings, and kids like Bowie were delighted because they were so foreign. Something has shifted in popular culture since Bowie, a shift stretching far beyond music to comprise Western tilting away from production and toward consumption. Creative anachronism now has internalized a punch-drunk lunacy, because the creativity lies in unlikely pairings rather than original scenarios. It needn't be this way.

Something new should always be possible.

Post-Genres and Acquisitive Philanthropy

It began with postpunk in the late 1970s. The Sex Pistols had burned out so spectacularly that it wasn't a stretch to conflate the group with the genre of punk as a whole. The Pistols' swift disappearance compelled fans and journalists to acknowledge the historical gap with a little prefix. "Postpunk" gradually came to embody traits that perpetuated punk's radical politics. Yet postpunk also described bands that, unlike the Pistols, weren't afraid to put forth something beautiful. The definitive postpunk act, Joy Division, is the classic example: tight, claustrophobic technique and recording conditions; lyrics that speak of alienation and fascist horrors; and intermittently, some of the most glacially beautiful music a mortal may be lucky enough to hear. The emphasis on the aesthetic was central here. Note the irony that Pistols' front-man Johnny Rotten reverted back to his original name John Lydon and started a new band, Public Image Limited, itself a prime example of postpunk. PIL's sound had little in common with the Pistols other than the shared quality of Rotten's/Lydon's voice. PIL was a fearless experiment in applying Brechtian mockery to dub reggae, and like Joy Division, it succeeded in strewing bleak landscapes with occasional delicacy and unearthliness.

Postpunk first emerged in the late 1970s and peaked in influence and market visibility in the first half of the 1980s. But the term and the musical style to which it pertains have never gone out of circulation. So, the Pixies' 1988 album *Surfer Rosa*, Kitchens of Distinction's 1991 album *Strange Free World*, and the Savages' 2013 album *Silence Yourself* have all been described as postpunk. There is ambiguity in such nomenclature. For postpunk can be understood as asserting that "punk", however defined, has ceased to exist. This is clearly belied by any number of self-professed punk bands that have operated since 1978, the year of punk's supposed death. Nevertheless, "postpunk" can mean "in the aftermath of", or even "in the ruins of" punk. The prefix can also communicate something more meditative. Punk may well continue to exist, but the "post-" in postpunk may refer to specific stylistic choices taken with punk aesthetics and history in mind. Postpunk is thus more historical, even Hegelian, proposing a retrospective "after the end of" punk. Whatever the slippages between these two meanings of postpunk, the prefix has since propagated itself throughout popular-music criticism. As early as 1998, Nelson George wrote of a post-soul nation, his description of hiphop's first generation of listeners.[158] The music of Mogwai and Sigur Rós and Godspeed You! Black Emperor, groups that usually jettison vocals and guitar solos and blues chords but otherwise maintain a rock sensibility, have been described as post-rock. (The author who allegedly coined the term "post-rock" is Simon Reynolds, whose work on retromania we have already discussed. Reynolds has also written a book on postpunk.[159]) And most recently, M.K. Asante, Jr. has written on what he calls the "post-hiphop generation", coming full circle to George's post-soul.[160]

What are the characteristics of a "post-" genre? These may recall traits often associated with late Beethoven: fragmentation and structural dismantling; reflection on the genre itself through lyrics or musical material; subverting expectations of the genre. These traits appear most noticeably in post-hiphop, which exists today simultaneously as a form of music and a discourse about hiphop's future as well as broader cultural issues. Kanye West's work, especially albums like *My Beautiful Dark Twisted Fantasy* (2010) and *Yeezus* (2013), are rooted in a catalog of hiphop clichés. The "diss" record, the misogynistic rant, the sample-driven rhapsody, the pushing of boundaries through appropriating from white high culture – all of these facets are here in West's corpus. J Dilla's *Donuts* (2006) comes across as a series of bagatelles, short tracks that flow from one to the next with no pause. I want to think about one track from *Donuts*, "Stop", which could stand as this type of late-period aesthetic of renunciation. It begins conventionally enough, with Dilla scratching over Dionne Warwick's "You're Gonna Need Me" (1973). Note that the formula here, of hiphop rapping set to a classic soul track, is the same as that in classic G-funk tracks like Dr. Dre's "Nothin' But A G Thang" (1992), which samples from Leon Hayward's gorgeous "I Want'a Do Something Freaky To You" (1975). But Dilla then stops the rapping and nearly all scratching and other interruptions to let Warwick's song play, uninterrupted, from 0:25 to 1:16. The only intrusions occur when Dilla inserts the odd "Yeah" rap – again, common enough since at least as far back as Public Enemy's *It Takes A Nation Of Millions To Hold Us Back* (1988), but newly intriguing in this context. For it is as if Dilla has stepped offstage for a moment in order to let Warwick's magisterial soul track reign. This is a moment similar to that in Duchamp or Warhol, where an object is so venerated for its own qualities that the artist appropriates it, more or less wholesale. "Stop"'s only significant deviation occurs at 0:58; Warwick and her backup singers say "You better stop", and then Dilla drops the volume only for a split-second before raising it back to normal. From this ravishing forest of vintage soul, Dilla extracts us, only momentarily. The effect is like withdrawal, immediate and painful.

We could perhaps interpret "Stop" conventionally as Dilla settling into a gem of a sample. But Dilla routinely digs up gems, and this moment strikes me less as relaxing than resigned. It could be heard as Dilla prefiguring Asante, who argues that hiphop has suffered from its associations with money and debauchery. There is something bigger than the music, a sense of beauty and justice that clings to the golden age of soul. Perhaps Dilla played the Warwick track out of admiration, or because he himself acknowledged the limitations and weaknesses of hiphop. If so, "Stop" can be counted as one of the most eloquent moments of post-hiphop.

Popular music is a perpetual-motion machine that produces novelty as a commodity. As Adorno notes, popular music changes superficial details of songs, but their underlying structure, format, and theme remain unchanged.[161] For Adorno, persistence overshadows the new in pop. Yet for Marx, capitalism is a perpetual-motion machine, and must by its nature continue to accelerate. There is no plateau or maintenance of present levels in capitalism. This may help explain why "post-" genres are currently so popular: it is contrary to the nature of pop capitalism for anything, a genre or an artist, to remain unchanged indefinitely. "Post-" genres exist because all genres are mortal. Still, post-genres contain something in addition to the never-ending fashion parade of styles. In the 1960s and 1970s,[162] most pop rhetoric spoke of the novelty of the artform, whereas the latent message in post-genres is reconsideration, retrenchment, and retrospection. This all is well-trodden territory, but the corollary is not: post-genres are premised on the idea that a genre has ceased to function, has even died out. Hiphop has been rife with calls for reform for over twenty years. The criticisms have originated from some obvious corners, journalists and academics who object to rap lyrics' misogyny or homophobia or racism or glorification of violence.[163] But the critiques have also been lodged internally. As far back as 1998, Lauryn Hill was crying out for hiphop conscience in tracks like "Doo Wop (That Thing)", which clearly distinguishes hiphop from older soul politics by contrasting Hills's strophic rapping with her soaring golden-soul choruses. The video for "Doo Wop" translates the conceit into the visual realm, splitting the screen into two halves that each portray a block party, one in the 1960s, the other in the 1990s. The 1960s-Hill is coiffed with the poise and beauty of Supremes-era Diana Ross. The 1990s-Hill is no less stunning, but her hair is worn naturally, and she's dressed in a tank top and shorts. Instead of the restrained gestures and choreography of Motown stars, Hill and her crew dance with rapid pivots and hip swaying. Hill's lyrics take to task the clichéd figures of hiphop: the thug who fronts a gangster's life but doesn't pay child support for his kids; the young black woman too beholden to white-imposed images of beauty to feel confident in her own body. On *The Miseducation of Lauryn Hill*, the album on which "Doo Wop" appears, Hill also lets loose barbs against former lover and Fugees-collaborator Wyclef Jean, as well as against the venality of hiphop. Against this concatenation of thwarted romance, music-industry shady dealings, and urban ills, Hill casts herself as an agent of change, a heroine capable of restoring hiphop, classic soul, and even reggae to speaking terms.

Even before hiphop conceived of its next reincarnation in so many words, there were signs that the music needed a foil. Common's "I Used to Love H.E.R." (1994) is an extended metaphor likening hiphop to a female lover. She begins as a mesmerizing beauty who is intelligent, assertive, and confident. She gains poise and sophistication and speaks of Black Power movements. Then she moves to LA, gets involved in the gangster scene, and compromises her principles. By the end of the track, Common tells us, she has sunk so low as to sell herself for money and publicity. A tragic allegory, no doubt, and made intimate through the elision with romantic love. Other jeremiads similarly despair of hiphop's prodigal ways by invoking God and righteous indignation. Jay Electronica's "Exhibit C" (2009) derides rival MCs for arguing "like Jews and Christians", while Electronica as a Five Percenter Muslim follows the right path. The sample here is Billy Stewart's slow soul ballad "Cross My Heart" from 1968. Meanwhile, Mos Def's 1999 "Fear Not Of Man", a milder, more optimistic call for hiphop (and humanity as a whole) to elevate itself, samples from venerated Nigerian Afrobeat polymath Fela Kuti's "For Not From Man" (1977). The thrust of these examples is that hiphop's intentions in sampling have shifted. During the 1980s and first half of the 1990s, MCs and producers vied to demonstrate hiphop's lineage in 1970s soul and funk. This was a gesture of desire and ambition, pointing toward what hiphop could achieve. But a shift has taken place in these examples, a defeatist admission that sonic affiliations to James Brown and George Clinton have failed to live up to 1970s progressive ideals. The sample, so critical to legitimizing hiphop in the 1990s, has since been coopted as a tool of post-hiphop. Through soul and Afro beats, post-hiphop asserts the decline of hiphop, not only for having sold its soul, but for having nothing of its own to compare with great works and acts of the past. It is notable that hiphop has, from its very beginnings, been predicated on an other, usually a musical other from the 1970s, from which it either draws inspiration or, in the case of post-hiphop, shows itself a defector.

Post-genres demonstrate that every genre communicates a message. Hiphop's message used to be one of protest and joy and competition, and later changed to materialism and sensuality. Post-hiphop's message is a lament that hiphop did not live up to its potential. So we end up with further proof that style and, in this case, genre have become more powerful than ever to the pop-music imagination. Post-genres expand the frame of discourse beyond the track or the few other tracks to which it refers, as well as beyond the artists who made the track. Just as style and genre have become intellectual properties and manipulable variables, they have also become guiding principles for *how* to think about a track, what to expect from it. And because we are contending with *post*-genres, we inevitably are led to see genres in decline.

With hiphop's "post-" incarnation, identity is still predicated according to a material presence. A well-chosen soul sample with minimal intervention can all at once honor the past and despair of the future; this is why Dilla's "Stop" and Electronica's "Exhibit C" are so eloquent. The narrative behind the genre of post-rock relies on absence rather than presence. As articulated in Mogwai's album *Mogwai Young Team* (1997), post-rock is (surprise!) a return to the roots of rock, a common-enough claim through the several iterations of 1950s-revivals.[164] But this return has nothing to do with the 1950s or rock 'n' roll, and everything to do with the strange one-offs and failed experiments that some early rock records contained, before the format of the genre was cemented by the recording industry. The quiet playfulness of Syd Barrett, the nocturnal quicksilver of Arthur Crudup's "That's All Right" – they serve as a beacon for Mogwai's instrumental meditations. In "Like Herod", a slow quiet vamp with drums, bass guitar, and self-effacing lead guitar suddenly erupts at 2:57 into an eleven-minute track, when the texture flares into a violent screech of feedback. Although neither Mogwai nor other mainline post-rock acts sound anything like jazz, they often sound as if they are thinking like jazz musicians. The default teleology of a rock song (say, by U2), in which verses, chorus, some instrumental flourishes, and a brief lyric all occur before the five-minute mark, is absent in Mogwai's music. Instead, there are extended passages of spinning riffs through different harmonic areas accompanied by varied rhythms. Imagine someone holding up a musical idea to the light, and turning it slowly to see it from all possible angles: this is Mogwai's compositional procedure. This could lead Mogwai dangerously close to the indulgences of the more bloated 1970s progressive-rock acts like Emerson, Lake, and Palmer. But Mogwai's melodic and harmonic language is kept relatively spare, commensurate with its instrumentation: usually just the basic guitars and drum combo, occasionally with understated cello or organ.

Post-rock, for all of its free experimentation, also possesses an outlook that verges on the post-mortem. After all, rock too has inscribed its own death into its history, most plangently in Don McLean's "American Pie" (1971), the crypto-dirge that talks of the day "the music died", when Buddy Holly, the Big Bopper, and Richie Valens died in a plane crash in 1959. Kevin J.H. Dettmar's book *Is Rock Dead?* brings up evidence supporting and negating the grim diagnosis, but that the question even need be posed only confirms that rock seems defunct; Dettmar points out that rock was being mourned as early as 1956![165] But consider that those bands and artists that are healthy in terms of their careers and that do play some sort of "rock" often have some prefix or prefatory word before that genre. Sunn 0))) is noise rock; Queens of the Stone Age is hard or stoner rock; Coldplay is alternative rock. There seems to be little desire to be just or listen to *just* a rock band. And this makes sense, because rock in its prime was a precarious and historically specific phenomenon of mostly white male musicians presenting stylized renditions of supposedly authentic black blues. Too much has happened in terms of history and politics for such a racial fantasy to persist. Now, white rockers couch their rock fictions in distant places (i.e. Sigur Rós in Iceland; Calexico in southwest border towns) or mythical themes (i.e. Sunn 0))) and Earth in the occult).

A post-script for this essay on post-genres: Phillip Sherburne published an article for the online popular-music site Pitchfork in April 2016 that spoke of the "EDM bubble".[166] This choice of term, seemingly innocuous, has staggering ramifications for our way of thinking about genre. The term "bubble" as it pertains to economics is defined as "a state of booming economic activity (as in a stock market) that often ends in a sudden collapse".[167] The Japanese economy from 1986 to 1990 experienced inflated stock and real-estate prices followed by drastic plummeting in value in 1991; the same occurred to the American real-estate market between 2006 and 2008, culminating in the 2009 recession. In financial parlance, calling an industry a "bubble" characterizes it as more than irrationally exuberant, to invoke former Fed chairman Alan Greenspan. It suggests that the entire activity is based on illusion or lies. So why call EDM's success a bubble? Sherburne presents a few isolated mentions in the press as far back as "way back in September 2013" (!) that refer to the oversaturation of EDM. This argument would seem to suggest that any genre that becomes popular enough to generate events in Las Vegas and to be featured in television commercials has sold its soul, which is certainly not a new argument. But to go from a critique of mass appeal to anticipating a collapse in financial or any other kind of value is a new development. To be fair to Sherburne, he is not alone in his assessment. I've taught a class on EDM for the past two years, and I've heard several students (who were connoisseurs of EDM) quip that EDM had replaced both hiphop and rock to become the quintessential music for "bros", a derogatory term for privileged white male college students; those same students said derisively that EDM's sudden displacement from the fringes to the mainstream had cost the music its quality. It is not unheard of for a genre to experience rapid mainstream acceptance before sudden public fall from grace; the Disco Demolition Night event at Comiskey Park in Chicago on 12 July 1979 popularized the phrase "Disco sucks" and exiled disco from American commercial radio within a few months. But to conceive of EDM as an economic bubble *in the present moment*, when it is still the favorite genre of twenty-somethings across the United States, is to conceive of a genre as possessing a lifespan, with decline and extinction as inevitable eventualities.

The extinction of one particular genre within EDM, rave or acid house, has become a normalized conceit. The 2006 Leyland Kirby album (presented under his stage name V/VM) *The Death of Rave* is a series of noise- and ambience-soaked tracks, all of which would be appreciated on their own merit as well-crafted electronica, without the aid of any extramusical reference. But the album title as well as the track titles, with names like "Machete's at the Banshee" and "Marple Libradome '91" refer to specific moments and locations in the history of rave culture in the UK. While the foreground of each track features mainstays of early twenty-first-century electronica like hazy drones and stomach-churning noise, the background intermittently contains traces of acid house like thumping, rapid kick drums and minimal hardcore basslines (e.g. perhaps one undeviating note throughout a track). This is what a rave sounds like if heard from a few miles away. Of course, Smith's album could remain at the personal level of a nostalgic reflection on the music and formative experiences of youth. But the trope of EDM's or rave culture's death has caught on: Mogwai released in 2014 the album *Rave Tapes*, and in 2011, the album *Hardcore Will Never Die, But You Will*.[168] And in 2011, Tim Hecker named his album *Ravedeath, 1972* after Kirby's album. There is also an electronic music label called Death of Rave. And let's not forget that the rave (and its descendant, the festival) has become a multi-million-dollar industry in the US since 2000. Not bad for a genre that has expired.

EDM is a large category for scores of niche genres, not all of which have existed simultaneously. It's precisely because of this stylistic overpopulation that death and post-mortem retrospectives are especially compelling concepts. All music is immediately available thanks to YouTube, and academia has rendered EDM into an object of study.[169] One means of making sense of this overabundance of recording product is to inscribe the expectation for death within the genre itself.

* *

The conclusion of Peter Brown's study of philanthropy in the latter years of the Roman Empire is breathtaking.[170] The Catholic Church rose to political and financial dominance thanks to support from less glorious corners of the Roman social hierarchy. Rich widows and newlywed brides, chafing at the friction between their wealth and Christ's admonition to the rich young man ("go, sell your possessions and give to the poor"[171]) gave generously to the Church. This was less drastic a change than it might appear, because philanthropy had already been expected from the Roman middle and upper classes. But pagan philanthropy was intended to benefit Rome, while early Christian charity was to benefit Roman Christians. Brown gives copious examples of gifts large and small: endowing a party, paying for a feast for a whole village, commissioning a plate or bowl. The triumph of Christianity had everything to do with redirecting this already-healthy sense of civic duty. Then, as now, church ladies were responsible for the unremarkable daily acts that keep a religious organization functioning.

Melodramatic though the metaphor may be, the music industry is undergoing its own collapse of empire. But as historians are quick to tell us, the Roman Empire did not fall suddenly, and even its gradual decline was accompanied by tendencies seemingly antithetical to collapse, like the concomitant civilizing of the very barbarians who stormed the empire. The "recording industry" is a broad term for what in fact was a specific and narrow set of circumstances: post-World War II disposable income in the hands of teenagers; gradual desegregation of American schools; the rise of Southern popular-music styles such as gospel, R&B, and country; and the rise of commercial recording labels. The industry might well have puttered along with artists drawing only local or regional audiences, were it not for the arrival of the industry's first cash cow, Elvis Presley. There had, of course, been recording superstars before Presley, from Victor Caruso to Hank Williams to Bing Crosby, but Presley embodied youthful rebellion, change in sexual mores, and white fascination with black culture in a way that drew previously unimagined numbers of listeners. The culture that Presley's success set in motion was driven by artist charisma, anxieties concerning race, and the divisive myth of teenage estrangement from adults. And these cultural factors were in turn abetted by the reliance on the physical phonographic object. Sound had to be inscribed on some tangible thing, whether shellac or vinyl disc, cassette tape, or compact disc. The act of purchasing the phonograph triggered ensuing thought-fictions, whether libidinal or generational or political. That piece of plastic gave the purchaser a lease on a fantasy life.

Some but not all of the special circumstances that made .the recording industry possible are still in place. Sex and youthful alienation continue to be marketable. Racial fantasies still abound. But the fact that recordings need no longer be material objects, and more devastatingly, that so much recorded music can now be heard for free through legal or illegal mechanisms, has changed the rules of engagement. Now, the fiction of the pop industry can be attained with no cost, which led to a panic in the early 2000s that the industry would collapse altogether.[172] But the industry has not collapsed, thanks in part to the fact that it has promulgated two new fictions: 1) There is too much music; and 2) Those who choose to buy music (when they could have it for free) become patrons of the arts. The first fiction refers to a solution that David Kusek devised around 2005, the "music-like-water" proposal, which treats the "whole" of recorded music less as an ocean of individual commodities than a public utility.[173] Consumers used to be told to think in terms of units like songs, albums, or artists. But as I've argued above, style has now become at least as important as any of these other units. And style necessarily entails an entire collection of works. The "music-as-utility" business model has flourished because it has normalized the fiction that there is too much music to let slip by, unappreciated. Subscription services like Pandora or Spotify are touted for their broad and deep catalogs. Their supposed asset is their host of algorithms for assembling suggestions based on a listener's preferences and listening history. This strategy works because it creates a false problem which it then solves. Although vast, the catalogs of Spotify are far from limitless. But by proffering a discrete yet slightly personal entity of the "playlist", it restores to pop music the false sense of intimacy that was burgeoning in the 1950s and 1960s. In paying an admittedly small monthly subscription, users are not only granted access to a whole ocean of material, but can rely on a guide to help them navigate that ocean.

It is no doubt thanks to subscription services and the music-like-water fiction that the recording industry is doing as well as it is, though record sales today are only a fraction of what they were at the beginning of the millennium. For younger consumers, especially, the idea of paying a pittance for instant music has become second nature. But Spotify does not have transparent procedures for ensuring that artists themselves are compensated in proportion to the frequency that their work is heard.[174] Cringe-worthy anecdotes describing major talent like Rosanne Cash receiving next to nothing for recently released material have alerted us to the fatal flaw of subscription services, that they benefit publishers and record labels far more than performers.

It is fashionable these days to protest outrages both serious and trivial. The outcry against Spotify will not likely trigger mass boycotts, but among a few self-proclaimed music aficionados, the rights of the artist have become a rallying cry. Capital is too clever not to jump on the opportunity to profit from social consciousness. Many listeners of niche genres, say electronica or Northern soul, choose to buy music even though they know that they could access it through Spotify or YouTube. These listeners sometimes explain their choice to pay as deriving from a sense of justice and civic-mindedness. Fans owe artists a fair living, this reasoning goes, and the decision to pay is a gesture with broad ramifications for entire communities. We should, in fact, focus on Bandcamp as a platform that has subtly built on this discourse of noblesse oblige. Think of what happens when one clicks on a track on Bandcamp. The first few times, the track plays immedi-ately. But in ensuing attempts (if the artist has calibrated the page to do so), any subsequent attempts to listen will result in a message stating, "It is time to open your heart (and purse)". A box asks the listener to pay for credit card or PayPal. If the listener does not pay, a little red heart appears onscreen, then shatters into pieces that fall to the bottom of the screen. Some artists allow a grace period of one or two additional listenings at no charge. But after, Bandcamp permanently blocks listening to the IP address of the computer accessing the site. Note also that those listeners who do buy music on Bandcamp can indicate their name and thumbnail image on the recording's page, as "supporters". This is analogous to donors who have their names listed in a concert program or building plaque. Publicly announcing one's philanthropy is hardly a new act. But this recent turn is groundbreaking, because it is in effect a highly targeted response to the transition of the music industry from one type of fetishism to another.

Make no mistake: there was never any objective use value in a music recording. The recording commodity began straightaway as a fetishistic commodity, whose exchange value was determined by the fantasies attributed to the music. The more highly accomplished the recording, the more evocative of escape or myth or fiction, the more units could be sold. In a short period of time, from the founding of Napster in 1999 to now, the entire recording industry has been devalued if we consider that payment is now optional. Those who practice "acquisitive philanthropy", who choose to give publicly as a gesture of self-aggrandizement as well as solidarity with artists, have replaced one form of commodity fetishism for another. Music now furnishes not only whatever private aesthetic thrills we imbue it with, but also the public satisfaction of a sense of belonging, of civic pride, of taste. This goes further than the phenomenon of "cultural capital", whereby people communicate their social class and education through the films, music, sports, and other cultural goods they consume.[175] It surpasses even Thornton's "subcultural capital", whereby underground cultural objects bestow their consumers with the special distinction reserved for those who reject the mainstream, however defined.[176] The capital at play is social capital, in fact an old phenomenon, as Brown's research demonstrates. In the late Empire just as today, the select few who can even afford to dispose of their money on such (let's face it) frivolous things as plates or tombs or arenas or music recordings changed not their desire to spend money, only the object of that spending.

* *

The idea that music of any kind, or specifically pop music, is dying out is a recognizably Hegelian one. "Popular music has become for us a thing of the past" – this is how Hegel might have phrased it today, with the inevitable historical evolution that such a statement implies. In fact, Hegel is probably the only thinker who could reconcile with sincerity the thought-fictions of pop's life and extinction. Pop is alive because it is evolving, so he might say, to the point of changing irrevocably into something else: heritage, fantasy, play-acting, or social ritual. The only problem with this line of thought is that it is belied by the facts. People continue to create, play, produce, purchase, pirate, and overhear popular music. Even though Bowie is dead, people listen to his music all over the world thousands of times a day. We can't go back, but we can go forward to the same material, the same habits. This perseverance suggests that the appropriate theorists here are rather Marx and Lacan. Marx gives us images of capital as a necromancer who wrests life and movement and work from dead or dying workers and objects. Capitalism relies, in fact, on images of the occult. What better way to evoke a frisson among customers than to propagate the myth of a dying art. But Lacan in turn gives us a way to destabilize Marx's cynicism. We may engage in popular music in ways reminiscent of the 1970s or 1980s, or even the 1890s. We do all of this with fetishistic disavowal, knowing that Bowie will never return, that cassette tapes were never that great in the first place, and that the pop industry will never revert to its robust state of a few decades ago.

And yet we repeat these rituals because they do the believing for us.

We are left with a dilemma of conviction. What do we believe, and how much do we want to believe it?

Conclusion: How to Recognize Demons

I have employed a methodology in this book that is open to criticism, especially from fellow musicologists. Some will object that I speak too generally, and mix discussions of popular music with glosses on philosophy. I may be accused of not being sufficiently rigorous, of simply proclaiming the existence of thought-fictions by fiat. But the most glaring vulnerability in these essays is that I use little in the way of "empirical evidence", that I seem to place myself as an omniscient arbiter who can discern between fiction and truth. Someone who sincerely believes that buying music is an act of charity rather than an exchange of goods for currency will not take kindly to my charge that we know that acquisitive philanthropy is a thought-fiction. But I do not, in fact, hold myself in such high regard as to believe that the gulf between reality and fiction is that discernable. I would like to think that Burton would agree that thought-fictions, like melancholy, are an occupational hazard for most humanists. All of the insulation of tenure and prestige cannot hide us from the fact that, from time to time, all of us teach or write of concepts that we can't quite believe in, in real life. And if we continue to fail to make research and teaching of import to those outside of our cliques, we do nothing but turn thought-fictions into myth.

All of us, artists and scholars and everyone else, know the holy moment when an artwork or view of nature or a beloved first open our heart. The rules of physical reality had been well-known, the cards laid out on the table... and then everything changes, even though we know that the outside world has not changed. I believe in musical fictions, perhaps not all those I have targeted here, but others, equally improbable and irreconcilable with reason. As an academic, I have consorted with even more outrageous thought-fictions – that music can convey lust, or madness, or a far-off region of the world – not for very long, just long enough to see my convictions for the threadbare shams they really are. I can be led to want to believe anything. Even if I don't fully believe it.

Style has served as the guiding thread in these essays because style in pop used to be our guide. A discretely helpful docent, style would tell us broadly what to expect from a song: how it would end, whom it would conscript, what fictional worlds it could conjure. I mourn popular-music style as it used to exist, because recent legal claims will rob it of that which we all have taken for granted in this ocean of music, a compass rose. When every single pop track is reduced to a piece of property that contains any number of smaller pieces of property, we have devolved into nominalism.

But let me return to the critique: who gets to say what is fiction? All of us do, because we do so everyday in ways that hardly seem courageous or noteworthy. For me, the Real moments (I capitalize the word to mean Lacan's sense of "real") happen most often early in the morning, when I first awaken. Cortisol levels in the brain are usually at their highest in the morning, which explains why it is common to feel anxiety and dysphoria upon getting out of bed. Whatever fantastical castles in the sky I had been constructing the night before, they fall to ruins in the dark just before dawn. My work is revealed as the farce I pretend not to know it to be. And the music I hold so dearly becomes unintelligible. Whatever secrets those sounds contain, I will never know. As the sky lightens and the cortisol levels recede, I gain hope, and my thought-fictions timidly re-emerge. And so it goes, day after day.

Lacan tells us that the Real is the authentic truth that we attempt to domesticate with language and culture. It's not necessary to claim that musical fictions have any sinister intent; they may, sometimes, but they may also simply be the grease that keeps the machine that is musical thought running smoothly, the ointment that helps us avoid the Reality that music is just sound.

For those of us lucky and mad enough to spend a lot of time thinking about music, any disruption of that fiction is unsettling, even shocking. That is, if we assume, with Lacan, a difference in value between reality and fiction. We should own up to reality, Lacan wants to say.

Marx is more pragmatic. Commodity fetishism is a forgone conclusion; what is not is how we treat ourselves and others on the basis of whatever illusory value we give to products. We should be aware of the fiction and then move on, Marx wants to say.

Of the three writers I invoked in Part I, only Hegel possesses what I would consider a healthy outlook on thought-fictions. Not only are they unavoidable, but they are themselves part of reality. Being and thought: the fundamental dialectic that undergirds all of Hegel's system. Being (and reality) are different from thought about being (and reality), and yet they are united in that difference.

All well and good, but how might such a Hegelian practice look, in real (Real) life? Even in a life frequented by thought-fictions? A hermit may give us a clue. At a critical moment in Athanasius' fourth-century hagiography, *The Life of Antony*, pilgrims visit Antony, who lives alone in the desert. Outside his barricaded dwelling, they hear the sounds of a mob in the midst of a battle. But they see no one when they peer inside through a window, and realize that demons are responsible for the noise. Antony then reassures them, saying "In this manner [...] the demons create apparitions and set them loose on those who are cowardly".[177]

Later, Antony teaches his fellow monks how to discern between demons and the presence of God:

For the discrimination between the presence of the good and the evil is easy and possible, when God so grants it. A vision of the holy ones is not subject to disturbance, for *he will not wrangle or cry aloud, nor will any one hear his voice* [...] The assault and appearance of the evil ones, on the other hand, is something troubling, with crashing and noise and shouting – the sort of disturbance one might expect from tough youths and robbers.[178]

Antony's wisdom extends deeper than any ability to ward off his visions. He learns to live with them. The first time that he was tempted with the illusion of an attractive woman, he trembled with fear and longing precisely because she seemed so real. Only after he weathered the temptation did Satan reveal himself as the force of "fornication" who leads so many astray. And after Satan's revelation, Antony deflects subsequent temptations with relative ease because he recognizes them as temptations, so much so that he can instruct his brethren as to their telltale traits.

The analogy I want to draw between Antony's visions and our musical fictions is not a perfect one. Thought-fictions pertaining to popular music are not particularly malevolent, and we do not have to struggle with them physically. But Antony's resignation to the fact that he will always be confronted with illusions and temptations is instructive. Like Antony, we cannot divest ourselves of these demons; they will return in some different form, but will return nonetheless. What we can do is follow the example of Antony's acolytes, by learning how to recognize musical fictions as they arise. The essays in this book are attempts to do just that.

Editors' Postscript

The real-estate tycoon Donald Trump was campaigning in the 2016 U.S. presidential election while Demers was finishing her manuscript. In retrospect, this campaign seems the harbinger of the United States' later move towards the far-right; we will speak more about this in a later book. For now, it pays to unpack the thought-fictions that Trump circulated: that the nation was weaker than it had been in recent decades, and that he would make the country great again. Trump, in other words, was dealing in two diametrically opposed fictions that together formed a dialectic of Digital-Age thought. Things are out of control, and things have never been more comprehensively organized. We are poor, and we are rich. We are dying, and we are evolving. For all of the idiocies of Trump's campaign, he was an unqualified success at normalizing ideas previously considered incompatible.

Thought-fictions of life and extinction are ways to confine what Lacan would term the "Real" knowledge, that music is merely sound – not meaning, not emotion, just sound. Vitality and extinction could be regarded as thought-fictions that gained momentum in the twenty-first century, that together brought order to the possibility and flux that is existence – no particular meaning or sense, just existence. But Demers cautions us not to fall into the trap of searching for antidotes to thought-fictions. The best we can do is be aware of them, and know when and how they inflect our thinking. Demers would likely have been distraught to see the eventual consolidation and elimination of humanities departments across North America, for she sincerely believed that the humanities, and her beloved Hegelian tradition in particular, offered the clearest path to such awareness.

We, in turn, can ask ourselves by what thought-fictions we govern our lives. What is the Real order that we rationalize, through language or commerce or distraction? What have we lost by mothballing disciplines deemed to be ornamental and irrelevant? Until we learn to examine the conditions for the possibility of our own thought, our demons will remain unseen, and all the more powerful for it.

Endnotes

Editors' Introduction

1 We thank our anonymous donor, a friend of a descendant of Demers, for the gift of the postcard and Demers' book manuscript.

Abstract

2 Farhad Manjoo, "Spotify Wants Listeners to Break Down Music Barriers", *The New York Times* (3 June 2015). http://www.nytimes.com/2015/06/04/technology/personaltech/spotify-sees-a-future-where-music-genres-dont-really-matter.html?_r=0.

3 Simon Reynolds, *Retromania: Pop Culture's Addiction to Its Own Past* (New York: Faber and Faber, 2011).

Part I: Thought-Fictions and Musical Style
Postcards and Thought-Fictions

4 M.R. Shetty, *Rhyming English Couplets* (New Delhi: Pentagon Press, 2012); Shetty, *Encyclopedia of Quotable Couplets* (New Delhi: Pentagon Press, 2005); Shetty, *Domestic Creatures: Poems* (Oxford: Oxford University Press, 1994).

5 Lon L. Fuller, *Legal Fictions* (Stanford: Stanford University Press, 1967), 1–6.

6 Fuller, *Legal Fictions*, 10.

7 Fuller, *Legal Fictions*, 9.

8 *Citizens United v. Federal Election Commission*, 558 U.S. 310 (2010).

9 In the 1888 decision Pembina Consolidated Silver Mining Co. v. Pennsylvania, the US Supreme Court ruled that the Fourteenth Amendment (which mandates equal protection under the law to all US citizens) applied to corporations as well as natural persons. *Pembina Consolidated Silver Mining*

Co. v. Pennsylvania, 125 U.S. 181 (1888).

10 Eric Posner, "Stop Fussing Over Personhood: Laws Treat Corporations (and Chimpanzees) As Persons Because It's a Useful – and Often Essential – Legal Fiction", *Slate* (11 December 2013): http://www.slate.com/articles/news_and_politics/view_from_chicago/2013/12/personhood_for_corporations_and_chimpanzees_is_an_essential_legal_fiction.html (accessed 25 May 2015).

11 David Foster Wallace, *This Is Water: Some Thoughts, Delivered on a Significant Occasion, about Living a Compassionate Life* (New York: Little, Brown and Company, 2009), 33.

Musical Fictions of the Past

12 Pierre Schaeffer, *Traité des objets musicaux: Essai interdisciplines*. Paris: Éditions du Seuil, 1966: 93–5; Joanna Demers, *Listening Through the Noise: The Aesthetics of Experimental Electronic Music* (New York: Oxford University Press, 2010), 26–7; Brian Kane, *Sound Unseen: Acousmatic Sound in Theory and Practice* (New York: Oxford University Press, 2014).

13 Michel Chion, *Audio-Vision: Sound on Screen*, trans. Claudia Gorbman (New York: Columbia University Press, 1990); Francisco López, "Schizophonia vs. l'objet sonore: Soundscapes and artistic freedom". Published in January 1997. http://www.franciscolopez.net/schizo.html (accessed 2 January 2016); Roger Scruton, *The Aesthetics of Music* (New York: Oxford University Press, 1997), 19; Jairo Moreno, *Musical Representations, Subjects, and Objects: The Construction of Musical Thought in Zarlino, Descartes, Rameau, and Weber* (Bloomington, IN: Indiana University Press, 2004), 50ff.

14 Mandy-Suzanne Wong, *Sound Objects: Speculative Perspectives* (PhD, UCLA, 2012); Joanna Demers, "Field Recording, Sound Art, and Objecthood", *Organised Sound* 14/1 (2009): 39–45; Brian Kane, "L'objet sonore maintenant: Pierre Schaeffer, Sound Objects and the Phenomenological

Reduction", *Organised Sound* 12/1 (2007): 15–24.

15 Edgar Sparks, *Cantus Firmus in Mass and Motet, 1420-1520* (Berkeley, CA: University of California Press, 1963), 65.

16 Christopher Page, *Discarding Images: Reflections on Music and Culture in Medieval France*, (Oxford: Clarendon Press, 1997), 17.

17 Alexander Rehding, *Music and Monumentality: Commemoration and Wonderment in Nineteenth-Century Germany* (New York: Oxford University Press, 2009); Lydia Goehr, *Elective Affinities: Musical Essays on the History of Aesthetic Theory* (New York: Columbia University Press, 2011), 136–170.

18 Andy Hamilton, *Aesthetics and Music* (London: Bloomsbury, 2007), 142–152; Goehr, *Elective Affinities*, 1–44; Steve Larson, *Musical Forces: Motion, Metaphor, and Meaning In Music* (Bloomington, IN: Indiana University Press, 2012).

19 Scruton, *The Aesthetics of Music*, 19.

20 Franz Brentano, *Psychology from an Empirical Standpoint*, trans. Tim Crane (New York: Routledge, 2014).

21 Scruton, *The Aesthetics of Music*, 17.

22 Marcel Proust, *Remembrance of Things Past. Volume 1: Swann's Way, Within A Budding Grove*, trans. C.K. Scott Moncrieff and Terence Kilmartin (New York: Vintage, 1981), 379–380. "Mais depuis plus d'une année que lui révélant à lui-même bien des richesses de son âme, l'amour de la musique était pour quelque temps au moins né en lui, Swann tenait les motifs musicaux pour de véritables idées, d'un autre monde, d'un autre ordre, idées voilées de ténèbres, inconnues, impéné-trables à l'intelligence, mais qui n'en sont pas moins parfai-tement distinctes les unes des autres, inégales entre elles de valeur et de signification." (Proust, *Du côté de chez Swann* (Paris: Flammarion, 1987), 484)

23 Proust, English translation, 381. "Swann n'avait donc pas tort de croire que la phrase de la sonate existât réellement.

Certes, humaine à ce point de vue, elle appartenait pourtant à un ordre de [486] créatures surnaturelles et que nous n'avons jamais vues, mais que, malgré cela nous reconnaissons avec ravissement quand quelque explorateur de l'invisible arrive à en capter une, à l'amener, du monde divin où il a accès, briller quelques instants au-dessus du nôtre." (Flammarion edition, 485)

24   Scruton, *The Aesthetics of Music*, 80.

Acknowledging Thought-Fictions

25   Stanley Rosen, *The Idea of Hegel's* Science of Logic (Chicago: University of Chicago Press, 2014), 174.

26   Plato, *The Republic*, trans. Desmond Lee (London: Penguin, 1987).

27   "Even the song of the bird, which we cannot bring under any musical rules, seems to contain more freedom and thus more that is entertaining for taste than even a human song that is performed in accordance with all the rules of the art of music: for one grows tired of the latter far more quickly if it is repeated often and for a long time. But here we may well confuse our sympathy with the merriment of a beloved little creature with the beauty of his song, which, when it is exactly imitated by a human being (as is sometimes done with the notes of the nightingale) strikes our ear as utterly tasteless." Immanuel Kant, *Critique of the Power of Judgment*, trans. Paul Guyer and Eric Matthews (Cambridge: Cambridge University Press, 2000), 126.

28   GWF Hegel, *Aesthetics: Lectures on fine art, Vol. 1*, trans. TM Knox (Oxford: Clarendon, 1975), 55.

29   GWF Hegel, *Lectures on the Philosophy of Art. The Hotho Transcript of the 1823 Berlin Lectures*, trans. Robert F. Brown (Oxford: Clarendon Press, 2014), 183.

30   Karl Marx, *Capital, Vol. 1*, trans. Ben Fowkes (London: Penguin, 1976), 163.

31 Marx, *Capital*, 168.

32 Marx, *Capital*, 167.

33 Marx, *Capital*, 189.

34 Marx, *Capital*, 190.

35 Marx, *Capital*, 198.

36 Marx, *Capital*, 255.

37 Marx, *Capital*, 308.

38 Marx, *Capital*, 314.

39 Marx, *Capital*, 342.

40 Marx, *Capital*, 332.

41 Marx, *Capital*, 931.

42 GWF Hegel, *Phenomenology of Spirit*, trans. A.V. Miller (Oxford: Oxford University Press, 1977).

43 Sigmund Freud, "Negation", in *Standard Edition, vol. 19* (London: Hogarth Press, 1994), 235–239.

44 Freud, "Negation", 236. My emphasis.

45 Jacques Lacan, "Introduction et réponse à un exposé de Jean Hyppolite sur la Verneinung de Freud", in *Le Séminaire, Livre 1: Les écrits techniques de Freud, 1953-1954*. 87–102 (Paris: Seuil, 1975).

46 Jean Hyppolite, "Commentaire parlé sur la 'Verneinung' de Freud, par Jean Hyppolite", in Jacques Lacan, *Écrits I*. 527–537 (Paris: Seuil, 1999).

47 Jacques Lacan, *The Seminar of Jacques Lacan, Book VII: The Ethics of Psychoanalysis, 1959-1960*, trans. Dennis Porter (New York: Norton, 1992), 252. Jacques Lacan, *Le Séminaire libre VII: L'éthique de la psychanalyse* (Paris: Seuil, 1986), 295: "Vos émotions sont prises en charge dans une saine disposition de la scène. Le Chœur s'en charge. Le commentaire émotionnel est fait. C'est la plus grande chance de survie de la tragédie antique – il est fait. Il est juste ce qu'il faut bêta, il n'est pas sans fermeté non plus, il est plus humain. Vous êtes donc délivrés de tout souci – même si vous ne sentez rien, le Chœur aura senti à votre place."

Fictions about Pop Style

48 Kiana Fitzgerald, "Beyoncé's 'Lemonade' Is Defiant In the Midst of Upheaval", NPR Morning Edition (25 April 2016). http://www.npr.org/2016/04/25/475542607/beyonce-defiant-in-the-midst-of-upheaval.

49 Hegel, *Aesthetics: Lectures On Fine Art, Vol. 1*, 163: "…art is the middle term between purely objective indigent existence and purely inner ideas."

50 Gary Tomlinson, *A Million Years of Music: The Emergence of Human Modernity* (Brooklyn, NY: Zone Books, 2015).

51 Matthias Mauch et al, "The Evolution of Popular Music: USA 1960-2010", *Royal Society Open Science*. 2:150081 (6 May 2015).

Rock and Performing Belief

52 Kim Gordon, "I'm Really Scared When I Kill In My Dreams (PiL)", *Artforum* (January 1983), reprinted at http://www.fodderstompf.com/ARCHIVES/REVIEWS/gordonritz.html (accessed 1 May 2016).

53 Greil Marcus, *Lipstick Traces: A Secret History of the Twentieth Century* (Cambridge, MA: Harvard University Press, 1989), 48.

Part II: Music Is Alive

54 Daniel J. Levitin, *This Is Your Brain On Music: The Science of a Human Obsession* (New York: Plume, 2006).

55 John Powell, *How Music Works: The Science and Psychology of Beautiful Sounds, from Beethoven to the Beatles and Beyond* (New York: Little, Brown, and Co., 2010); Oliver Sachs, *Musicophilia: Tales of Music and the Brain*, rev. ed. (New York: Vintage, 2008); Joshua Leeds, *The Power of Sound: How to Be Healthy and Productive Using Music and Sound*, 2nd ed. (Rochester, VT: Healing Arts, 2010).

56 Georgina Born, *Rationalizing Culture: IRCAM, Boulez, and the Institutionalizing of the Musical Avant-Garde* (Berkeley: UC

Press, 1995).

57 Douglas Kahn, *Earth Sound Earth Signal: Energies and Earth Magnitude in the Arts* (Berkeley: UC Press, 2013).

58 John Croft, "Composition Is Not Research", *Tempo* 69/272 (April 2015): 6–11.

59 Susan McClary, *Feminine Endings: Music, Gender, and Sexuality* (Minneapolis: University of Minnesota, 2002); Carolyn Abbate, "Music—Drastic or Gnostic?" *Critical Inquiry* 30 (Spring 2004): 505–536.

60 Charles Taylor, *Sources of the Self: The Making of the Modern Identity* (Cambridge, MA: Harvard University Press, 1989).

61 Sigmund Freud, *Introductory Lectures on Psychoanalysis* (Liveright: Standard Edition, 1989).

62 Quentin Meillassoux, *After Finitude: An Essay on the Necessity of Contingency*, trans. Ray Brassier (London: Continuum, 2008); Graham Harman, *Towards Speculative Realism: Essays and Lectures* (Winchester, UK: Zero Books, 2010).

63 Timothy Morton, *Hyperobjects: Philosophy and Ecology After the End of the World* (Minneapolis: University of Minnesota Press, 2013).

64 Jane Bennett, *Vibrant Matter: A Political Ecology of Things* (Durham: Duke University Press, 2010).

65 Eugene Thacker, *After Life* (Chicago: University of Chicago, 2010).

66 N. Katherine Haynes, *How We Became Posthuman: Virtual Bodies in Cybernetics, Literature, and Informatics* (Chicago: University of Chicago Press, 1999).

67 Reza Negarestani, *Cyclonopedia: Complicity with Anonymous Materials* (Melbourne: Re.Press, 2008).

68 Hegel, *Lectures on the Philosophy of Art*, 191.

69 Hegel, *Aesthetics: Lectures on fine art, Vol. 1*, 164.

70 Hegel, *Lectures on the Philosophy of Art*, 191.

Suffering Music

71 Kim Cascone, "The Aesthetics of Failure: 'Post-Digital' Tendencies in Contemporary Computer Music", *Computer Music Journal* 24/4 (Winter 2000): 12–18.

72 Demers, *Listening Through the Noise*, 73–78.

73 Demers, *Listening Through the Noise*, 84–89.

74 Demers, *Listening Through the Noise*, 92–93.

75 Compare this to, say, Dr. Dre's "Ain't Nothin But A G-Thang" (1992), which samples Leon Haywood's "I Want To Do Something Freaky To You" (1975). Dre makes the Haywood sound perfectly at home in its new G-funk surroundings.

76 Joanna Demers, *Steal This Music: How Intellectual Property Law Affects Musical Creativity* (Athens, GA: University of Georgia Press, 2006), 28.

77 Edmund Burke, *A Philosophical Enquiry into the Origin of Our Ideas of the Sublime and Beautiful* (Oxford: Oxford University Press, 1990).

78 Paul Virilio, "A Pitiless Art", in *Art and Fear*, trans. Julie Rose. 27–65. (London: Continuum, 2003).

79 [Editors' note: Demers' arguing for a non-human subjectivity resonates oddly with her mention in Part I of the legal fiction legitimized by the Citizens United decision, that corporations possessed personhood under the law.]

Change and Evolution

80 Tom Barnes, "Scientists Just Determined the Most Important Genre of Music of All Time", Music.mic. http://mic.com/articles/117628/this-scientific-study-of-17-904-songs-just-revealed-the-most-important-genre-in-history#.eF3l0J2Tp (accessed 5 May 2016).

81 Matthias Mauch, Robert M. MacCallum, Mark Levy, and Armand M. Leroi, "The Evolution of Popular Music: USA 1960-2010", *Royal Society Open Science* 2: 150081 (2015), pg. 1. To distinguish from the authors' other article, I will hence-

forth refer to this 2015 article as "Mauch/MacCallum (2015)".

82 Mauch/MacCallum (2015), "The Evolution of Popular Music", 2.

83 Mauch/MacCallum (2015), "The Evolution of Popular Music", 1–2.

84 Charles Darwin, *The Origin of the Species* (New York: Signet, 2003).

85 Mauch/MacCallum (2015), "The Evolution of Popular Music", 4.

86 Mauch/MacCallum (2015), "The Evolution of Popular Music", 4.

87 Darwin, *The Origin of the Species*, 9–41.

88 Robert M. MacCallum, Matthias Mauch, Austin Burt, and Armand M. Leroi, "Evolution of Music by Public Choice", *Proceedings of the National Academy of Sciences of the United States of America* 109/30 (24 July 2012): 12081-12086. To distinguish from the authors' other article, I will henceforth refer to this 2012 article as "MacCallum/Mauch (2012)".

89 MacCallum/Mauch, "Evolution of Music By Public Choice", 12084 and passim.

90 MacCallum/Mauch, "Evolution of Music By Public Choice", 12085.

91 MacCallum/Mauch, "Evolution of Music By Public Choice", 12081.

92 Charles Darwin, *The Descent of Man* (London: Penguin, 2004), 638–639.

93 Bennett Zon, "The 'non-Darwinian' revolution and the Great Chain of Musical Being", in *Evolution and Victorian Culture*, eds. Bernard Lightman and Bennett Zon, 196–226 (Cambridge: Cambridge University Press, 2014), 220.

94 Alex Mesoudi, *Cultural Evolution: How Darwinian Theory Can Explain Human Culture and Synthesize The Social Sciences* (Chicago: University of Chicago Press, 2011), 38.

95 Zon, "The 'non-Darwinian' revolution", 209, 221.

96 Gary Tomlinson, *A Million Years of Music: The Emergence of Human Modernity* (Brooklyn: Zone, 2015), 41.

97 Luigi Luca Cavalli-Sforza and Marcus W. Feldman, *Cultural Transmission and Evolution: A Quantitative Approach* (Princeton: Princeton University Press, 1981).

98 Mesoudi, *Cultural evolution*, 26.

99 Simon Reynolds, public lecture at USC Doheny Library, lecture in MUHL on 6 December 2013.

Style Is Intellectual Property

100 Adam Rutherford, *Creation: The Future of Life* (London: Penguin, 2014), 48–49.

101 Demers, *Steal This Music*; Alex Sayf Cummings, *Democracy of Sound: Music Piracy and the Remaking of American Copyright in the Twentieth Century* (New York: Oxford University Press, 2013).

102 17 U.S.C. §102 (2012).

103 David J. Moser and Cheryl L. Slay, *Music Copyright Law* (Boston: Cengage, 2011), 28.

104 Moser and Slay, *Music Copyright Law*, 33.

105 Moser and Slay, *Music Copyright Law*, 33.

106 Mazer v. Stein, 347 U.S. 201, 217 (1954).

107 Copyright Act of 1976, Pub. L. No. 94-553, §301(a), 90 Stat. 2541, 2572.

108 Kembrew McLeod and Peter DiCola, *Creative License: The Law and Culture of Digital Sampling* (Durham, NC: Duke University Press, 2011); Siva Vaidhyanathan, *Copyrights and Copywrongs: The Rise of Intellectual Property and How It Threatens Creativity* (New York: NYU Press, 2003).

109 410 F.3d 792 (6th Cir. 2005).

110 *Copyright Law – Sound Recording Act – Sixth Circuit Rejects De Minimis Defense To The Infringement of a Sound Recording Copyright. – Bridgeport Music, Inc. v. Dimension Films, 383 F.3d 390 (6th Cir.2004)*, 118 Harvard Law Review 1355, 1356

(2005).

111 *Bridgeport Music, Inc. v. Dimension Films*, 230 F. Supp. 2d 830, 839 (M.D. Tenn. 2002).

112 *Bridgeport Music, Inc. v. Dimension Films*, 383 F.3d 398 (6th Cir.2004).

113 *Bridgeport Music, Inc. v. Dimension Films*, 383 F.3d (6th Cir.2004), at 399.

114 *Williams v. Bridgeport Music, Inc.*, No. LA CV13-06004 JAK, 2014 WL 7877773.

115 Michael T. Ghiselin, *Metaphysics and the Origin of Species* (Albany, NY: SUNY Press, 1997), 149.

116 John Seabrook, *The Song Machine: Inside the Hit Factory* (New York: Norton, 2015), 201.

117 Allan F. Moore, Allan F., "Categorical Conventions in Music Discourse: Style and Genre", *Music and Letters* 82/3 (August 2001), 441.

118 Reynolds, *Retromania*, 278–279.

119 Gottfried Toussaint, "Classification and Phylogenetic Analysis of African Ternary Rhythm Timelines", Extended version of paper that appeared in *Proceedings of BRIDGES: Mathematical Connections in Art, Music, and Science*, University of Granada, Granada, Spain, June 23–27, 2003, pg. 25–36. http://cgm.cs.mcgill.ca/~godfried/rhythm-and-mathematics.html (accessed 26 March 2016).

120 See, for instance, the map featured in Alex Jennison, "5 EDM Genres That Will Take Over America", Into the AM (http://blog.intotheam.com/5-edm-genres-take-over-us/), 11 February 2014 (accessed 8 May 2016).

121 Ghiselin, *Metaphysics and the Origin of Species*.

122 *Association for Molecular Pathology v Myriad Genetics, Inc.*, 133 S Ct 2107 (US 2013).

123 133 S. Ct. (US 2013) at 2116.

124 Teige P. Sheehan, "The Supreme Court Holds Genes Are Patent-Ineligible Products of Nature," *NYSBA Bright Ideas*

22/2 (Fall 2013), 3.

125 Hegel, *Lectures on the Philosophy of Art*, 191: "[…] the work of art is certainly nothing animated, and, since there is nothing just externally alive, the living thing is higher than what is lifeless. However, there is no work of art with respect to this aspect of being just a thing, for the work of art exists only as spiritual, as having [192] received the baptism of spirit; it portrays something spiritual, something shaped in harmony with spirit. Therefore the product of art is from spirit and is for spirit, and it of course has superiority in that the natural product, though a living thing, is something transitory, whereas the work of art is something abiding, something permanent."

126 Negarestani, *Cyclonopedia*, 5.

127 Negarestani, *Cyclonopedia*, 129.

Part III: Music Is Dying Out

128 Seabrook, *The Song Machine*, 295.

What We Lost In Losing Bowie

129 Bonnie Malkin, "David Bowie: Astronomers give the Starman his own constellation", http://www.theguard ian.com/music/2016/jan/18/david-bowie-astronomers-give-the-starman-his-own-constellation (accessed 1 April 2016).

130 *Ziggy Stardust and the Spiders From Mars*. Dir. D.A. Pennebaker, 1973.

131 Some might object that the Tin Machine projects are an important exception.

132 "To have no manner has from time immemorial been the one grand manner, and in this sense alone are Homer, Sophocles, Raphael, Shakespeare, to be called 'original'." Hegel, *Aesthetics: Lectures On Fine Art, Vol. 1*, 298.

133 In "Scott Walker Radio Interview 1984 (2 of 4)", Walker speaks of his mid-1970s albums (before *Nite Flights*) as a

series of sins for which he had to do penance. https://www.youtube.com/watch?v=X4SjXIl8Bjc (accessed 12 May 2016).

134 Really! – in the track "Clara" on the album *Drift* (2006).

135 In "Brando".

A Society for Creative Anachronism

136 Reynolds, "The Shock of the Old: Past, Present and Future in the First Decade of the Twenty-First Century", in *Retromania*, 403–428.

137 In using the term "creative anachronism", I refer to the Society for Creative Anachronism (SCA), an international organization devoted to the recreation of mostly European medieval history. This group is distinguished from other historical reenactment groups (some of which Reynolds discusses: *Retromania*, 44–54) by its acknowledgment of the imaginative nature of its activities, and drew much of its inspiration from the novels of J.R.R. Tolkein. One measure of the influence of creative anachronism on general culture is the success of George R.R. Martin's series of fantasy novels, *A Song of Ice and Fire*, and the HBO television series based on those novels, *Game of Thrones*. Martin has stated that *A Song of Ice and Fire* is loosely based on real events of the "War of Roses", the fifteenth-century English wars fought between the rival Lancaster and York houses. *A Song of Ice and Fire* is recognized as a high-point in creative anachronism. "The Real History Behind Game of Thrones, Part I", https://www.youtube.com/watch?v=ZyszuqFQIss (accessed 16 May 2016).

138 [Editors' note: Italics added.]

139 Personal correspondence, 18 March 2016.

140 *Portlandia*, "Dream of the 1890s", https://www.youtube.com/watch?v=0_HGqPGp9iY (accessed 16 May 2016).

141 Nick Hornby, *High Fidelity* (New York: Riverhead, 1995),

88–89.

142 Joanna Demers, *Drone and Apocalypse: An Exhibit for the End of the World* (Winchester, UK: Zero Books, 2015), 80–83.

143 To be fair, the same is true of vinyl records that are played too many times.

144 Carol Vernallis, *Unruly Media: YouTube, Music Video, and the New Digital Cinema* (New York: Oxford University Press, 2013).

145 Such a defense was eloquently put forward in McClary, "Living To Tell: Madonna's Resurrection of the Fleshly", in *Feminine Endings*, 148–168.

146 Joanna Demers, "Accents in Some Recent Digital Media Works", in *The Oxford Handbook on Digital Audiovisual Media Aesthetics*, eds. Amy Herzog, Carol Vernallis, and John Richardson. 140–153 (New York: Oxford University Press, 2013).

147 Rhapsody of Fire, with Christopher Lee, "The Magic of the Wizard's Dream," https://www.youtube.com/watch?v=Eh42GbHcKws (accessed 16 May 2016).

148 "What I sing is symphonic metal […] It is actually very, very good indeed." Interview with Christopher Lee (10 November 2011), https://www.youtube.com/watch?v=9Tdl021ArsM (accessed 12 April 2016).

149 Fredric Jameson, *Postmodernism, or, The Cultural Logic of Late Capitalism* (Durham, NC: Duke University Press, 1992).

150 Michel Houellebecq, *La possibilité d'une île* (Paris: Fayard, 2005), 145.

151 "El Mundo interviews Sigur Rós, October 2002", http://sigur-ros.co.uk/media/intervi/elmundo0.php (accessed 16 May 2016).

152 *Game of Thrones*, Season 4, Episode 2.

153 Hugo Ball, "Karawane", https://www.youtube.com/watch?v=z_8Wg40F3yo (accessed 16 May 2016).

154 Kurt Schwitters, "Ursonate", https://www.youtube.

com/watch?v=Kk-3W3c9Svg (accessed 16 May 2016).

155 John Higgs, *The KLF: Chaos, Magic and the Band Who Burned A Million Pounds* (Croydon, UK: Phoenix, 2012).

156 The KLF, *The Manual: How To Have A Number One Hit – The Easy Way* (KLF Publications, 1988).

157 The KLF, "The Rites of Mu", https://www.youtube.com /watch?v=nRTGfx0z-nc (accessed 16 May 2016).

Post-Genres and Acquisitive Philanthropy

158 Nelson George, *Hip Hop America* (New York: Penguin, 1998).

159 Simon Reynolds, *Rip It Up and Start Again: Postpunk 1978-1984* (New Your: Penguin, 2004).

160 M.K. Asante, Jr., *It's Bigger Than Hip Hop: The Rise of the Post-Hiphop Generation* (New York: St. Martin's Griffin, 2009).

161 Theodor W. Adorno, "Perennial Fashion – Jazz", in *Prisms*, trans. Samuel M. Weber. 119–132 (Boston: MIT Press, 1967).

162 Reynolds, "Out of Space: Nostalgia for Giant Steps and Final Frontiers", in *Retromania*, 362–398.

163 Jamilah Evelyn, "To the Academy with Love, From a Hip-Hop Fan", *Black Issues in Higher Education* 17/21 (December 7, 2000): 6; Hua Hsu, "Foucault's Turntable: Hip Hop Scholars Bumrush the Academy", *The Village Voice* (January 8–14, 2003).

164 Reynolds, "Rock On (And On) (And On): The Never-Ending Fifties Revival", in *Retromania*, 276–310.

165 Kevin J.H. Dettmar, *Is Rock Dead?* (London: Routledge, 2005).

166 Phillip Sherburne, "Popping The Drop: A Timeline of How EDM's Bubble Burst", *Pitchfork* (5 April 2016), http://pitchfork.com/thepitch/1086-popping-the-drop-a-timeline-of-how-edms-bubble-burst/ (accessed 19 April 2016).

167 "Bubble", fifth definition. *Merriam-Webster's Collegiate Dictionary*, 11th ed. (Springfield, MA: Merriam-Webster, 2012).

168 Hardcore was a type of fast tempo, minimal acid house popular at UK and European raves during the early 1990s.

169 "The Best Universities for Electronic Dance Music, 2014". https://thump.vice.com/en_us/article/the-best-universities-for-electronic-dance-music-2014 (accessed 19 April 2016).

170 Peter Brown, *Through the Eye of a Needle: Wealth, The Fall of Rome, and the Making of Christianity in the West, 350-550 AD* (Princeton: Princeton University Press, 2013).

171 Matthew 19: 16–30.

172 Joanna Demers, "Music, Copies and Essences", in *The Sage Handbook of Popular Music*, eds. Andy Bennett and Steve Waksman, 584–597 (London: Sage, 2015).

173 David Kusek, "Music Like Water", *Forbes* (31 January 2005), http://www.forbes.com/forbes/2005/0131/042.html (accessed 19 April 2016).

174 Seabrook, *The Song Machine*, 296–297.

175 Pierre Bourdieu, *Distinction: A Social Critique of the Judgment of Taste*, trans. Richard Nice (London: Routledge, 2010).

176 Sarah Thornton, *Club Cultures: Music, Media, and Subcultural Capital* (Hanover, NH: Wesleyan University Press, 1996).

Conclusion: How to Recognize Demons

177 Athanasius, *The Life of Antony and The Letter to Marcellinus*, trans. Robert C. Gregg (Mahwah, NH: Paulist Press, 1980), 41.

178 Athanasius, *The Life of Antony*, 58. Emphasis in original.

In the Dust of This Planet
Horror of Philosophy vol. 1
Eugene Thacker
In the first of a series of three books on the Horror of Philosophy, In the Dust of This Planet offers the genre of horror as a way of thinking about the unthinkable.
Paperback: 978-1-84694-676-9 ebook: 978-1-78099-010-1

Capitalist Realism
Is there no alternative?
Mark Fisher
An analysis of the ways in which capitalism has presented itself as the only realistic political-economic system.
Paperback: 978-1-84694-317-1 ebook: 978-1-78099-734-6

Rebel Rebel

Chris O'Leary

David Bowie: every single song. Everything you want to know, everything you didn't know.

Paperback: 978-1-78099-244-0 ebook: 978-1-78099-713-1

Cartographies of the Absolute

Alberto Toscano, Jeff Kinkle

An aesthetics of the economy for the twenty-first century.

Paperback: 978-1-78099-275-4 ebook: 978-1-78279-973-3

Malign Velocities

Accelerationism and Capitalism

Benjamin Noys

Long listed for the Bread and Roses Prize 2015, Malign Velocities argues against the need for speed, tracking acceleration as the symptom of the on-going crises of capitalism.

Paperback: 978-1-78279-300-7 ebook: 978-1-78279-299-4

Meat Market

Female flesh under Capitalism

Laurie Penny

A feminist dissection of women's bodies as the fleshy fulcrum of capitalist cannibalism, whereby women are both consumers and consumed.

Paperback: 978-1-84694-521-2 ebook: 978-1-84694-782-7

Poor but Sexy

Culture Clashes in Europe East and West

Agata Pyzik

How the East stayed East and the West stayed West.

Paperback: 978-1-78099-394-2 ebook: 978-1-78099-395-9

Romeo and Juliet in Palestine
Teaching Under Occupation
Tom Sperlinger
Life in the West Bank, the nature of pedagogy and the role of a
university under occupation.
Paperback: 978-1-78279-637-4 ebook: 978-1-78279-636-7

Sweetening the Pill
or How we Got Hooked on Hormonal Birth Control
Holly Grigg-Spall
Has contraception liberated or oppressed women? *Sweetening
the Pill* breaks the silence on the dark side of hormonal
contraception.
Paperback: 978-1-78099-607-3 ebook: 978-1-78099-608-0

Why Are We The Good Guys?
Reclaiming your Mind from the Delusions of Propaganda
David Cromwell
A provocative challenge to the standard ideology that Western
power is a benevolent force in the world.
Paperback: 978-1-78099-365-2 ebook: 978-1-78099-366-9

**Readers of ebooks can buy or view any of these
bestsellers by clicking on the live link in the title. Most
titles are published in paperback and as an ebook.
Paperbacks are available in traditional bookshops. Both
print and ebook formats are available online.**

**Find more titles and sign up to our readers' newsletter at
http://www.johnhuntpublishing.com/culture-and-politics
Follow us on Facebook at
https://www.facebook.com/ZeroBooks
and Twitter at https://twitter.com/Zer0Books**